The Miller's Daughter

The Story of Ara

D1528048

CANDACE CUBITO

Dedicated to
Joe, Kristen, Vito, Paul, Chrissy, Annalee, Claudia, Micky,
Vito, Roman
I love you all.

Ara is the daughter of Peter, the miller, and Amelie, the finest spinner in Belstrumburg. She learns to spin and weave from her mother. It is a simple, happy life until tragedy strikes, and her father utters the fateful words, "My daughter can spin straw into gold." The story of Rumpelstiltskin has existed for hundreds of years. In all this time people have thought of him as the villain, but they are oh, so very wrong.

Table of Contents

CHAPTER 1

"Ara, don't dawdle. We're going to plant thread today," Amelie called upstairs from the keeping room. She was making porridge in the small caldron over the fire, her long skirt sweeping the ashes as she stirred.

Ara ran downstairs. "Mama, did you say we are planting thread?"

"I did." She smiled.

Ara laughed. "That's silly. We can't plant thread. Nothing can grow from thread. Threads aren't seeds."

"Yes, I am being a little silly. We're going to plant flax seeds this morning which will eventually become linen thread. So hurry with your breakfast. It's best to do the planting while the ground is still dewy."

Ara paused, tilting her head. "Wait. I hear Jana at the window. He's late today." She hurried back upstairs to her bedroom. A few minutes later, she descended the stairs with a large, shiny black bird on her shoulder. "Amelie!" it squawked and flew to Amelie's arm, nestling under her chin.

Amelie planted a kiss on Jana's head and nuzzled it. "Where have you been, my friend?" She cut off a small piece

1

of dried apple and fed it to the bird. "I have some seeds for you. Go to the hutch and get them." The raven flitted over to a plate and began to peck at it. She always kept some seeds or food scraps on the bottom shelf for Jana who arrived early each morning, typically pecking at Ara's bedroom shutters to wake her up. "Amelie love. Amelie love," he said.

Sunlight streamed into the room through the large unshuttered window. Two chairs stood at attention at either end of a wooden table centered in the room. A small bench sat under it waiting to be used. The blue painted hutch against the wall was taller than Amelie. It held three drawers for utensils and cloths, and its upper shelving stored the plates, bowls, and cups.

Amelie bent down to kiss her daughter's head. The little girl pulled out the bench and sat before the bowl of porridge her mother had scooped for her. "Here, you forgot your pillow," offered her mother as she scooted it under Ara's bottom. "That's better."

"Look, Mama." Ara removed the pillow and sat down again at the bench. "I'm growing, and now I can reach the bowl." Her mother examined her. It was true. She had grown several inches in the last months. How had she not noticed?

With breakfast finally finished, the mother and child left the house with cloth bags of flax seed slung over their shoulders. As they started their trek to the waiting field, Jana flew out the window and up to the top of the tallest apple tree. "Goodbye, Ara," he called. "Goodbye, Amelie."

"See you later, Jana," they waved their daily ritual. The bird flew around them twice and went off on some adventure.

"Where does he go?" wondered Ara aloud.

"I don't know, to catch some bugs and find some carrion, I suppose. He always comes back, though. That's the important thing."

"How old was I when he started coming to the house?"asked Ara, slipping her hand inside her mother's. A wisp of hair strayed into her eyes, so Amelie tucked it behind her daughter's ear.

"Actually," her mother spoke softly, "he has been with me since I was just about your age."

Ara stopped walking and stared at her mother. "Mama, you never told me that! No wonder he loves you more than me."

"Oh, that's not true. I found him lying on the ground when he was just a baby and nursed him until he was well. He's been with me ever since."

"How did you know how to take care of him?"

"I had a friend who helped me and we learned together. We took turns catching bugs and gathering seeds. Jana was a very hungry little bird, just like you when you were a baby." She gave her daughter a small tweak on the nose which resulted in giggles.

"Where is the friend now?"

"My friend stayed behind when I moved in with my aunt and uncle, and Jana came with me." Amelie became quiet.

Ara knew the story of her mother's family, but her father cautioned her not to ask questions about it. "It is too sad for her," he had whispered in her ear.

They were nearing the field in the back of the house just behind the apple and pear trees. A large kitchen garden was in the front of their cottage. Seedlings were just sprouting in the upturned dirt. To the left was a coop with a dozen chickens squawking and pecking at the ground, and to the right was a small barn and enclosure for the horse and two nanny goats. The nannies trotted out to greet them, bleating as they walked past. Amelie reached into her apron and took out two apples, handing them to Ara who tossed them to the goats. "Good morning, Gertie. Hello there, Ursula."

They stopped at a freshly tilled plot in the front of the field. Ara inhaled the scent of the loamy soil. It smelled of spring and, vaguely, of horses. "This is how to sow the seeds. Watch." Amelie leaned to one side and heavily distributed the seeds onto the ground. "Now you do it." Ara laughed and flung the seeds into the wind, watching them settle onto the raked ground. "That's not quite right, Daughter. They need to be sown close together so they can help each other grow up straight and tall. Watch me again." The young girl stood still observing her mother, and then began sprinkling the seeds closer together. "There you go. You are officially farming."

It was a large plot, big enough to keep Amelie busy spinning thread and weaving all winter. When they were finished, Ara examined their work and turned to her mother. "Won't the birds eat all the seeds?" she asked.

"They will eat some, but Jana will help keep watch over it. Besides, we're not quite done." Her mother picked up the wooden rake she had used to loosen the soil. "I'm going to tamp down the seeds with the back of the rake. That will settle them down into the ground. You are just the right size to walk on them. Your shoes will do the same job as the rake. Don't stomp on them; just walk lightly."

"Like this, Mama?" Ara walked delicately over the newly seeded ground.

Her mother's mouth curled up as she watched her. "Just like that."

"We're putting them to bed," Ara whispered.

After several minutes of tamping and walking, Amelie put her hands on her hips and surveyed their work. "We're done here. Let's go see Papa at the mill."

The mill squatted by the side of the river near the edge of the village of Belstrumburg. Peter Miller called it the Old Man because it was ancient and sagging and bearded with ivy. His father ran the mill before him, and his grandfather before that. The miller didn't own the mill. It belonged to the village, or rather to Lord Belstrum who controlled the village.

All the peasants used the grist mill and the miller was given a "miller's toll" as payment. It was dusty, hard work. The miller had to open the sluice to let the paddlewheel turn which would turn the millstone that ground the grains against a stationary bed. He would raise or lower the millstone depending on how fine or coarse the grain needed to be. The grain would be hoisted up in sacks and emptied into bins in order for it to drop into a hopper and down to the millstone. After it was ground, the flour would be collected into sacks for the peasant to take home. Wheat, barley, and rye were the primary grains ground by Peter, his assistant and apprentices.

The mill stood several cottages away from their own. As Ara neared it, she scampered ahead of her mother, her dark hair streaming behind her. "Papa, Papa," she shouted. When he heard her calling, he went to the door and opened his floury arms to embrace her.

"Hello there, my little spider," he laughed, planting a kiss on her forehead. He raised her up and gave her a big hug before setting her down again.

"Ewww. Why did you call me a spider?" she asked, sweeping the flour and grain from her dress. The air was filled with flour particles that settled, unnoticed, in her hair.

Her father laughed again and bent down so he was eye level with her. "Because," he explained, "one day soon your mother will be teaching you to spin flax into linen thread and then weave it into fabric. That's just what spiders do, spin and weave."

"But spiders are ugly. I'm afraid of them," she protested, screwing up her face.

Peter stroked her cheek. "Spiders are our friends. They eat the bad insects that destroy our crops. I am thankful for them every day. All the peasants are, too. Besides, their webs are strong. Wind and rain can't destroy them. You will make threads and linens that are as strong and thin as spider silk, too."

Amelie walked into the mill. She looked past the dust covering her husband and only saw the man who had loved her since she moved to her aunt and uncle's village ten years ago. He was kind and strong with a broad back and hands the size of trencher plates. Under his cap his hair was still as blonde as when they met, though perhaps a little thinner. His apron encircled a thickening waist that told of the plentiful food a miller could afford.

His eyes crinkled when he saw her. She was the most beautiful woman he knew with her chestnut hair and blue eyes flecked with green. "Well, this is a fine treat to have you visit."

"Ara did her first planting of flax seed so I decided to reward her with a visit to see her papa."

"Well, lucky you did." The miller bent to Ara, putting his hands on his knees. "I believe I saw a whale swimming in the river this morning. Let's go see if we can find him."

"A whale?" Ara's eyes widened as she slipped her hand into her father's big fist. She tugged at him as he led her to the river. Rocks along the bank caused small rapids in the fast flowing current.

When they reached the riverbank, Peter made a show of searching for the whale, shading his eyes with his hand and scanning broadly. Suddenly he pointed by the rocks. "There!" he shouted. "There's the whale's blow!"

Ara squinted and looked where he pointed. She saw the water splashing upward from the rocks. Maybe that was it. Her eight-year-old mind could conjure up the whale. "I see it!" She hopped around like a rabbit, clapping her hands. She ran over to her mother who was standing back from the river's edge. "Mama, I saw a whale. He's over there!" she cried, pointing.

Amelie smiled. Her husband was always making up stories that their little girl believed. He had convinced her that their nanny goats could fly at night and that a goblin lived under the chicken coop. They were harmless enough stories. "A whale! My, that's quite something to have a whale swim all the way up our river from the sea."

She looked over to her husband and shook her head slightly. There you go again, she had motioned. "Time for us to go. Let's go check for eggs and milk the nannies."

Ara ran back to her father and gave him a squeeze. "Mrs. Becker brought some honey, yesterday. I'll make you something sweet," she promised, and left him at the mill's door.

On the walk back to their house, Ara turned to her mother. "Mama, whenever you sell your linen, the women say it is the best in the village. Will I be able to make such fine fabric when I am older?"

Mother and daughter walked towards their home. "Yes, you will indeed. I have a few secrets to make my linen softer and lighter. I will teach them to you."

Ara brightened. "Goody. I want to make the best, just like you. Did your mama teach you?"

"Yes, she did. She was a wonderful weaver. She said to weave the best linen, one needs the best thread, and to have the best thread, one needs the best flax."

"Did we plant the best flax today?"

"We did, indeed. I always look for the finest flax plants in the field and save them for the seeds."

When they reached their cottage, Jana was perched upon the chimney and called to them. They looked to the top of the half-timbered home. "If you give me a kiss," called Amelie, "I will give you a little piece of meat I've saved for you." The bird flew down and landed on her head. "Come to my shoulder, you little fiend. You are ruining my coif." She readjusted her cap.

Jana hopped down to her shoulder as they entered the house. "Mama," asked Ara. "How many days will it take for the flax to grow?"

"Mmmm, it takes about one hundred days," answered her mother, distracted as she reached for the egg basket at the top of the cupboard.

"I do not know how to count that high."

Her mother reached for another basket. "Here. Every day put one pebble in the basket until you have ten. Then take them out and put in..." She looked around. "Just a minute." She hurried into her weaving room and came back with a small bundle. "Look, I've cut up some fabric pieces for you.

When you have ten pebbles," she instructed, "take them out and put in one piece of fabric, and then start over. When you have ten pieces of fabric in the basket, it will be time to harvest the flax."

Ara looked at her mother solemnly. "I will not forget. Every morning when I get up, I will add one pebble to the basket."

"Yes, that's good. Now, let's go check on the eggs and milk our nannies."

"And find ten pebbles."

Amelie laughed. "And find ten pebbles."

CHAPTER 2

7 WEEKS LATER

The sky was a big gray blanket, quickly darkening to black. The storm would be strong. Quickly Ara and her mother closed up the shutters and ran out to the nannies. They hurried them into the barn and then raced to the chickens who squawked and fluttered as they were hustled into the coop. Large drops began pelting them as they reached the door to the house. "Whew," said Amelie. "We made it just in time."

A clap of thunder boomed and Ara ran into her mother's arms, whimpering. "We're fine, Daughter. We're inside and safe."

"What about Jana?" sobbed Ara. "Will he die out there?"

"He'll be fine, but let's go see if we can call him in. I think he's in one of the fruit trees." Mother and daughter ran upstairs to open the shutter in Ara's room. The rain began streaming onto the floor as they began calling. "Jana! Jana! Come to the house!"

The bird flew from the tree to Amelie's outstretched arm. Quickly Ara slammed the shutters closed and ran to get rags to soak up the puddle that had formed on the floor. "Good boy," she said handing a rag to her mother. "You had us worried. Stay here until the storm is over."

Jana hopped to the bed and shook his feathers, sprinkling water over the quilt Ara had helped her mother make last winter. She gathered him up and patted him dry. "Let's go downstairs and get you by the fire."

Her mother busied herself putting a stew into the caldron. The room soon filled with with the mingling aromas of lamb and onions and garlic. Ara sat on the stone floor playing a game of jacks, and Jana flitted to and fro, from the cupboard where he pecked his food to the floor near Ara. The rain was battering the roof. Amelie peeked through the shutters. "This storm is going to last for hours. This is a good time to teach you to spin."

"My very first lesson on the spinning wheel! Oh, yes." Ara scrambled to her feet, put away her game and ran over to the wheel, but her mother stopped her and carried it farther into the keeping room. "We'll need a little more space for both of us." She pulled up her spinning stool. "Sit on my lap."

Ara felt the steady beating of her mother's heart as she settled herself in. "Now, this tall stick with the fibers on it is called a distaff. While I treadle the wheel, I'm going to make the thread and it will spin onto the bobbin here," her mother explained pointing to each object. "I'm going to treadle today because it's hard to learn two things at once, but you are going to draw the fiber into the thread." Her voice changed. "Look at me."

Her daughter twisted around to look at her mother's soft face. "Your thread will not be as good as mine. I have been spinning for many years and have much practice. My thread was lumpy and bumpy when I first learned. You should expect that yours will look that way, too. Be patient with yourself and you will get good over time. Understand?"

"Yes, Mama. Just like I made a messy bed when I first learned, but now my bed looks neat."

"Yes, just like that. Now, see this water here?" She pointed to the bowl she kept at the base of the spinning wheel. "We have to wet the fingers on our right hands." Both dipped their hands to just above their palms, shaking off the excess. Her mother continued. "The flax is sticky. When your fingers are wet, they smooth out the fibers and make it stronger."

Amelie readjusted her daughter on her lap. "Watch me. See how I keep my right hand on the thread and pull? I do it very gently. We have good flax so the fibers will be long." She pulled at the fibers and kept a steady rhythm with the wheel. The unkempt fibers turned into fine, thin strands of thread filling the bobbin. "Now, my left hand is busy keeping the fibers in place. You try to pull with your right hand and I will guide you."

Leaning forward, Ara placed her right hand on the fibers and pulled. "Good," said her mother. "Just a little more gently." Ara eased up and the thread became thinner, though still a bit lumpy. They worked that way, silently, rhythmically, until the distaff was empty and the bobbin was full, with Ara stooping every so often to wet her fingers

"Look at this thread. You did a much better job than I did the first time I spun." She gave her daughter a tight squeeze and kissed her head. "You must be part spider."

Ara climbed off her mother's lap and grinned. "Papa said I would become a spider." She danced around. "I'm a spider. Look at all my legs!"

"All right, my little spider," Amelie laughed. "Let's get ready for supper. Papa will be home soon."

Peter Miller patted his belly. "Amelie, that was a fine meal. The tenderest mutton I've ever had, and the taste was a little different." He reached across the table and covered her hand with his large, calloused one. "Is it a special occasion I've forgotten?" He studied her. Her chestnut hair was a contrast to his, and her blue eyes sparkled below her dark brows.

"Nothing grand. Your sister said I should try adding rosemary to the stew," said Amelie. She slipped her hand from under his and gave it a pat. "We'll be back to beans and cabbage tomorrow." She rose and began clearing the table. "Are you off?"

"That I am." He stood and collected the bread trenchers. He gave them out to beggars or stray dogs as he strolled down to the tavern several times a week to have a couple of pints with the men. "It was busy at the Old Man today. Many of the peasants are bringing in their stored grains to make room for the harvest. It'll be like this for a spell."

"Mind that you don't have more than a couple of pints," she warned. "That night you came back banging at the door scared me mightily."

"Ah, Ami, my love, that was a score ago, and I learned my lesson. I could barely hoist up the sacks the next day." He hung his head and then looked up impishly. "But I'll be fine tonight and back early enough to have some fun with you." Grabbing her from the back, he spun her around and tilted her back giving her a long, lusty kiss.

"Go on now," she shooed him with her cloth towards the door.

The next morning Ara jumped out of bed when she heard Jana croaking at the window. When she came downstairs, she was surprised to see her father breaking his fast. "Papa, you are still here." She gave him a hug. He put her on his lap and shared his porridge with her.

"Oh, I just thought I would stretch a bit in bed this morning," he said winking at his wife. "But I need to get on." He lifted her up as he rose and sat her back in his chair. "Finish up my bowl." He strode over to the door, grabbing his cap off the hook. "The Old Man is calling me." With a flourish and a bow to Amelie, he took his leave.

Her mother was kneading dough that she would bring to the village oven later. "How many pebbles are in the basket?"

"Let me count." She walked over to the hutch and looked into the basket. There are four pieces of fabric and eight pebbles."

"So how many days has it been since we planted the flax?" asked her mother.

"Let me see. Ten, twenty, thirty, forty and eight. Forty-eight days."

"Good girl." Amelie was proud of how bright her daughter was. "Run off to the coop and bring in the eggs. When you get back, we'll go out to the flax together."

Weeding was a tedious task for an eight year old. The plants came up above her ankles. It didn't take Ara long to begin complaining. "This is hard. Why didn't we do this when the plants were smaller?"

"If we weed when the flax is shorter, it may break, so we have to wait until they are this tall to be strong enough. Work at this a little longer and then I'll have you go feed Gertie and Ursula."

A half hour later, Amelie leaned on her hoe and patted her wet forehead. "Okay, little one, go feed the nannies. You can feed the chickens, too. I'll be back at the house in a bit."

Ara was playing with her rag doll when her mother came in walking gingerly. She jumped up. "Can we spin some more thread?"

"Oh, Daughter, let me sit for just a bit." Her hair was matted and damp and there were stains under her arms. "It's a hot one today. Your father brought some water from the spring this morning. Will you bring me a cup of it, please?"

After drinking, she put her head down on the table. "I'm a bit exhausted today. It must be the heat."

"Mama, are you unwell?" Ara frowned. She had never seen her mother this tired.

"I...I'm not sure." She raised her head and winced. "Ara, run to Aunt Clare and ask her to come here."

Trembling, Ara bolted out the door and ran as fast as she could to her aunt's cottage a few doors away. Clare Cooper was stooped in the kitchen garden picking the early peas.

"Aunt Clare!" she yelled. Startled, the woman stood upright. "Something is wrong with my mother!" Ara's chest was heaving.

The two of them hurried back to the house, tears streaming down the little girl's cheeks. They found Amelie doubled over on the chair.

"Heat up some water," commanded her aunt. She turned to Amelie. "Can you walk upstairs?"

"I don't think so," she grimaced. Blood was spreading across the back of her dress.

Clare helped her to the floor. Keeping her eyes on her brother's wife, she ordered Ara, "Go get your father."

"What's wrong with Mama?" she cried.

"Just go get your father!"

Her heart pounding, Ara sped off. Her legs couldn't carry her fast enough, and she tripped, falling hard to the ground.

Scrambling to her feet, she didn't notice that her hands and chin were scraped. She was breathless by the time she reached the mill. When Peter saw his daughter, his face paled. "Mama," was all she could utter.

"Sig, take over," he ordered his senior worker. He thrust Ara onto his back and raced to the house.

Peter threw the door open and spied his wife lying on the floor next to a pile of bloody rags. He rushed to her side, cradling her in his arms. "Amelie, Amelie," he murmured, his lips in her hair.

Her blue eyes brimmed with tears. "I lost the baby," she cried, turning her face into his chest.

"Baby?" He looked over at Clare.

"She was just a few months along." She nodded slightly. "She'll be all right. Get her to bed."

Putting one hand under her legs and the other across her back, he scooped her up and carried her upstairs. Ara started to follow, but her aunt put her arms across the girl's shoulders. Quietly she said, "Your mama needs some time with your papa." She eyed her niece, noticing her scrapes for the first time. "Let me clean you up." Gently she dabbed at Ara's hands and chin with a rag wet with wine.

Scanning the room, she spotted the doll and handed it to her niece. "Here, you hold your dolly while I clean up." She busied herself scrubbing the blood off the floor and washing the basin. She threw the rags in the fire.

A while later, Peter trudged down the stairs. "Clare, I thank you." He ran his hand wearily through his hair.

"Tosh, Brother. She's your wife."

He shook his head. "I didn't even know she was carrying a baby."

"Amelie already lost two others. She wanted to wait a bit longer before she told you." She put down the kitchen rag and wiped her hands on her apron. "I'll send Jasper along later with some supper for you and broth for Amelie."

Peter walked his sister to the door. "That would be a kindness."

He felt Ara pull on his apron. "Can I go see Mama?" She looked like a little puppy pleading to be petted.

He lifted her up into his arms. "Mama is resting now. We'll look in on her later."

"Mama was going to have a baby?" She wiped his cheeks with her hands.

"Yes, little girl."

"But now she's not?"

"No." Both were quiet for awhile. He set her down. "Let's go check on the nannies. They may need milking."

They spent the rest of the day together, each in quiet contemplation. They milked the nannies, and tended the garden. The radishes and fennel needed some weeding, and they set out some tansy to keep the insects at bay. "Remember to deadhead these," he pointed to flowers. "If you don't, they will spread all over the garden."

Then they went out to the flax field and finished weeding. Ara sighed soundlessly. She was tired and wanted her mama, but said nothing. Jana flew around overhead but didn't come down. Later when they checked on Amelie, they found her asleep with the raven perched on the bedside table. "Jana is keeping watch over his best friend," Peter whispered. They left them together.

Ara woke up in her bed late the next morning still in her clothes. She didn't remember falling asleep in her father's lap.

CHAPTER 3

Ara tiptoed to her mother's bedroom doorway. She could see her sitting up with her eyes closed in the four poster bed. "Mama?" she called tentatively.

Her mother turned her head toward the doorway and motioned her in. "Come up on the bed, Daughter."

She clambered up the bed steps and into her mother's waiting arms. "I missed you, Mama." Ara was a miniature of her mother, fine boned with dark hair and blue eyes with the same specks of green scattered around the pupil.

Her mother gave her a squeeze. "I missed you, too. You were a brave girl getting help for me yesterday."

"Are you all better now?" She stayed within her mother's clasp, holding her breath.

"Much better, little one." Ara blew out through her mouth. "I'm going to rest a little longer. Go on downstairs. Papa said Aunt Clare brought some biscuits over this morning."

"Are you getting up today?"

"In a while. Today I need you to tend to the animals."

"Should I milk Gertie and Ursula?"

"Papa already did it."

"All right." Ara eased herself from her mother's hold and hopped down from the bed. "Mama, Jana didn't wake me up today."

"He stayed with me all night. When Papa opened the shutters this morning, he flew away. He's probably somewhere nearby. Call for him when you go outside."

Ara spread butter on a biscuit with her fingers and ate it slowly. This was a strange day. Mama wasn't downstairs and no one ever brought them breakfast before. She grabbed the egg basket from the hutch and went to the barn for the feed. Following her daily routine helped keep her from worrying about her mother.

Ara was teaching her doll how to cook with her miniature pots and pans when she heard footsteps above. She leaped from the bench and met her mother at the bottom of the stairs. Amelie was still in her nightgown and her hair was uncombed. "Good morning, Mama," Ara said shyly, turning from side to side.

Amelie took her hand and together they walked to the table. "Oh, I see you are cooking with Lucie."

"I'm teaching her to make porridge. Would you like some?"

Amelie nodded and Ara pretended to feed her. "Delicious. You're a good cook." Ara beamed.

"There are biscuits from Aunt Clare if you're still hungry."

"I'm fine for now."

"Can we do some spinning today?"

"We'll do some tomorrow. Why don't you put your toys away and grab the slate? I'll teach you to write your name."

Ara's face lit up as she clapped. She scurried around putting away her toys in the basket by the hutch and retrieved the slate and slate pencil along with a rag.

"Up on my lap," her mother patted. When Ara was settled, she showed her how to draw two slanted lines and another straight across them. "Now you try it."

Ara held the pencil awkwardly, and with tongue between her lips, she made a shaky letter A. She looked at her mother uncertainly.

"That's a very good try. Here, hold the pencil like this." Her mother adjusted the writing instrument in her daughter's hand. "Try it again."

Slowly Ara formed the A. "Good girl. That's a pretty letter. Now let me show you R."

Together they worked through the three letters in Ara's name.

Ara put down the pencil and took Amelie's hand. She held it close to her face and examined the ring on her mother's finger. "This looks like a shiny piece of wheat."

"Yes, that is exactly what it is, golden wheat," said her mother. She gently removed her hand from her daughter's grasp. "Let me show you something else." Amelie pulled at her necklace trapped under her nightgown collar. "Take a look at this."

Ara scrutinized the thick, round gold disc hanging from a delicate chain. "It's beautiful," she breathed, "and it has the letter A on it." She looked up at her mother. "A for Ara!"

Her mother chuckled. "Well, my name starts with an A, too. It's actually an A for Amelie."

Ara brightened. "We have the same first letter."

"We do. When you are older, I will give you this necklace," her mother promised.

Ara grinned broadly. "How old will I have to be?"

Mrs. Miller bent her head to her daughter's forehead. "Older."

As the months flew by, Ara grew more adept at spinning. Her mother gave her the short flax fibers to practice on and, with time, the bumpy linen thread smoothed out. Her mother set her daughter's bobbins aside to be weaved into fabric for work clothes. Peter didn't need anything fancy, and he liked to show off his daughter's handiwork.

"Look at this fine apron. She's filling so many bobbins now, the weavers can make make enough fabric for ten aprons," he exaggerated.

The village men at the tavern humored him. He was a good man who laughed easily at their jokes, and was an honest miller. Besides, he was more well off than many of them and was known to pay for a round or two of ale on occasion. "Here you go, lads," he would say. "This one's on me."

They were careful, though, not to let him imbibe too much. Sometimes they would catch each other's eyes and one would say, "Can we take you up on that tomorrow, Peter? I've a lot of tilling to do and my horse expects straight furrows," or some other likely excuse. They needed a sober miller in the morrow, and Peter's weakness was drink.

It was a convivial group of peasants and merchants who headed to the tavern regularly, although not as frequently as Peter. The beamed ceiling was low and dark and the tables were roughly hewn. The men sat on benches and talked of work and weather and taxes and tithes. "The bishop wants more from us again even though the tithing barn is full. He is squeezing us dry."

"Between the taxes and the tithes, we barely have enough to get by, yet the bishop wants more money to build a new chapel for the king."

The biggest complaint was about the king, but it was whispered low by an old peasant. "Guendel was rich under King Phillip II. Then when King Manfred reigned, he spent enormous amounts of our tax money making Lundgrin Castle the grandest in Europe. We all had to tie our breeches tighter. Now King Richard wants to make it grander. We can't afford more taxes." The others nodded in agreement.

The merchants commiserated with the peasants. If there wasn't enough money in their pockets, there wasn't enough to spend in the shops. The only one who kept quiet was Peter Miller because he milled the grains whether they came from the peasants, the lord of the village or the church. The miller's toll remained the same.

All the peasants lived within the village wall for safety's sake and took their wagons into the fields each morning. A few of them owned their lands, but most rented from the lord. It was a hard life. The peasants' wives worked in the fields along with their husbands, bringing their children with them.

As the miller's wife, Amelie's life was easier by comparison. She tended her kitchen garden, her small flax field, and the goats and chickens, but she had more time than other women to tend to her daughter and her home. She had a small business weaving her linen thread into fabric. She kept her loom in the back room on the first floor of the cottage. Because her spinning was superior to others in the village, her fabric was as well. She sold it to Mr. Kaufmann, the wealthiest merchant in the village. He paid her fairly and his customers paid a dear price for it. She occasionally spun and weaved for some of the peasants' wives who would bring her their flax. Although the work was the same, as a charitable woman, she charged them far less.

When Ara was young, her mother kept her just outside the doorway of the weaving room, because the fibers often filled the air. She kept bowls of water in the corners of the room to add moisture to the threads. Ara would sit and play with her dolly or spinning top. Sometimes Jana kept her company, although most days he flew off after breakfast. As Ara got older, her natural curiosity brought her into the room. "What is that?" She pointed to the object her mother was pushing through the threads.

"That's called a shuttle," answered her mother.

"It looks like a little boat," laughed Ara.

"So it does." Amelie smiled.

"What does it do?"

"It carries the weft through the warp."

"What is the warp?" On went Ara's questions with her mother patiently answering.

Finally her mother asked if she would like to push the shuttle back and forth. Ara quickly agreed and they spent the afternoon weaving together. Over time Amelie began setting up the thread for her daughter who began weaving small projects.

CHAPTER 4

One morning as Ara came down the stairs with Jana on her shoulder, her mother sat her on one of the chairs at the table. They were reserved for her parents, so she knew something special was about to happen.

"You are in your twelfth year," began her mother, "and now you are a young woman."

Ara looked at her expectantly, and her mother continued. "I have promised you something." She handed her daughter a small linen bundle. "Open it."

Puzzled, Ara peeled back the layers of cloth. Her mouth opened and her eyes widened. "Mama!" she gasped. "Your necklace!"

"No, Ara, *your* necklace." She picked up the necklace nestled in the cloth, and put it around her daughter's neck.

Ara's eyes sparkled. "Oh, Mama, thank you." She hugged her mother tightly. "This is the best gift I have ever received."

Her mother held her at arm's length and looked at her. "It looks beautiful on you."

"May I go show Frieda? I won't be gone long."

"No," came the reply. "This is just between us. Here," Amelie pulled Ara's smock open slightly at the neck and dropped the pendant against her skin. "Wear it tucked inside your clothes. Keep it against your heart. It will remind you how much you are loved."

Ara put her hand up to the center of her chest and felt the hard lump. "Yes, Mama."

It was a breezy midsummer morning when Amelie and her daughter headed out to the field. The pretty blue flowers had disappeared and the flax was yellowing at the bottom. "It won't take long to harvest. The roots are shallow, so we'll just pull them out like this." She stooped and grabbed the flax near the ground. Just as promised, it released easily. Ara had been helping to gather the crop for a few years now, but she tolerantly listened to her mother. Together they pulled the stalks out by the roots and laid them on the ground.

They worked steadily, grabbing small clumps at a time. Leaving a small patch of flax for the seed heads to mature, they tied the stems into sheaves. These bundles were then set vertically, seed heads up, in groups of six to eight, resting against each other in conical shapes.

Amelie stood back and admired them. "This is a fine crop. We have more stooks this year than any I can remember." By the time she and Ara finished, the sun was almost overhead. "It's a blessing to me that you are tall and strong. You have saved me several hours of work." They both wiped their brows with their sleeves.

Mother and daughter headed back to the house, arms entwined for a well deserved long drink. "How will we know when the stooks are dry?" wondered Ara.

"We'll begin checking in a few days. They're dry when the stalks turn white. I used to get brown stalks at first, but by saving the best seeds over the years, I now get white ones." Amelie looked sideways at Ara. "Goodness, I don't mean to show pride, but white means it's the best flax."

"You work hard, Mama. You can be proud every once in awhile. But I'll make the sign of the cross for you." Ara touched her forehead, chest and shoulders and kissed her forefinger up to the sky.

On Sunday, the Miller family prepared for church. Ara and her mother put on clean smocks and kirtles. They each donned a gown, lacing it up on the sides. They picked up the front of the gowns and attached it at their waist, exposing both the contrasting lining of the gowns and the red of their kirtles. Peter was waiting for them downstairs in a clean shirt and breeches. "Here are my beautiful ladies," beamed Peter. He had a spoon in his hand and was standing near the porridge simmering in a pot over the fire.

"Don't eat anything before mass," reminded Amelie. She examined her husband and slipped her arm through his. "You clean up nicely."

After the church sermon, the Miller family mingled with the congregants. Ara went off one way to be with her friends. They didn't have much opportunity to visit with each other during the week. Peter and several of the men formed a circle to discuss the sermon about the difference between venial and mortal sin, while Amelie and a few neighboring women exchanged pleasantries. Mr. Kaufmann caught up with Amelie. "Good morning Mrs. Miller. It's a hot one today."

"Why hello, Mr. Kaufmann," Amelie smiled. "Yes, it is hot indeed. It's a good day to relax in the shade on the Sabbath."

"I have some news for you."

"Good or bad news, Sir?" She was pleased to see him. An easy acquaintance had formed over the years.

"On the whole it is good news. One of the servants from the manor was in my shop yesterday. She told me her Lady had been gifted some linen fabric from my shop and sent word that it was most pleasing to her.

Amelie blushed and put her hand to her chest. "Oh, why that is lovely news. It is always nice to hear a kind word about one's work."

Mr. Kaufmann continued. "She purchased the rest that I had and she wants more as quickly as possible."

"I am all out of fabric and thread and have just stooked my flax a few days ago. It takes a good deal of time and work to prepare the linen. Retting alone takes six weeks to soften the stalks, four if we have wet weather. Then they need to be dried again before I can use the break on them. After that..."

The merchant broke in. "Isn't there a way to speed up the process?"

Amelie hesitated. "Well, yes. If I ret the flax in water, the soak will only take about a week, ten days at most. The problem, though, is that if I put it in the pond, it ruins the water and smells foul."

Both were quiet for a moment. Then Mr. Kaufmann spoke. "What if you retted the flax in the river? The water moves constantly and therefore would have no odor."

She considered it. "Why, yes," she said slowly. "I believe that will work." Then with more enthusiasm, "Yes, it will indeed."

"Good then," the merchant grinned. "We have a solution."

"One thing, though. I will need some flat rocks, let us say this big,'" she motioned with her hands, "to weigh down the sheaves of flax. Can you hire a man to have them by the river nearest me when I am ready for them?"

"I promise. They will be there before the week is out."

"Then you shall have your linen in half the time."

When the flax stooks were dry, Amelie and Ara carried a table and rippler to the field. "Now, before we can begin retting, we have to remove the seeds. These are immature ones, so we can't use them for planting, but Jana and the chickens will enjoy eating them. See the teeth on the rippler?" Her mother pointed to the block of wood with iron teeth sticking straight up from the base. Ara nodded. "We are going to put handfuls of stalks between the teeth and pull. This will remove the seed heads. Let me put this cloth down to collect them."

They worked as a team through the morning, untying the bundles and rippling the stalks. The seed heads fell to the cloth and crunched under their shoes. When they had finished, her mother scooped the seeds into a bucket. Ara walked to the patch of flax and pulled out the stalks which had been left for the seeds to mature, while her mother settled the canvas cloth back on the ground.

"These are the seeds we'll put away for next year. Do you remember how we separate the seeds from the chaff?"

Ara giggled. "It's my favorite part. We dance on them!"

"We sure do. When we're done, we'll put them in this cloth bag." Amelie patted the sack strapped across her chest. She quickly pulled the flax through the teeth. Then the two of them joined hands, dancing and stomping on the seed heads.

"Whew! I'm hungry," announced her mother after the seeds were in the bag. "Let's put the rippler away and eat. We'll begin the retting tomorrow." Before they left, they remembered to leave a few seeds on the ground for the fairies.

Amelie decided she would ret half the bundles on the ground, and the other half would soak in the river for a week. Half would yield enough for the Lord's wife.

She reviewed her plan with Ara after supper when Peter left for the tavern. "We'll do our chores here at the house first, and then I'll go to the field for the flax. I'll start opening and spreading half of the sheaves out while you get the wagon. When you get to the field, we'll load the rest of the bundles and take them down to the river. Bring some rope, too."

Jana pecked at Ara's window in the morning. "Ara," he called.

"Hello, my friend," she greeted him, stroking his black feathers. "Mama and I are very busy this morning. Want to meet us in the field?"

The raven croaked and flew to an apple tree as she hurried downstairs to eat a hasty breakfast. Quickly the two of them tended to the early morning chores, and then Ara went to hitch up the wagon and horse while Amelie headed to the field. By the time her daughter arrived, she had unbundled several sheaves and spread them on the ground close to one another. Together they finished laying out the sheaves until half of them were on the ground.

"Now, let's put the rest in the wagon." As they walked to the river leading the horse, Jana circled above croaking softly. "He is curious about what we're doing," said Amelie.

"Did you ever ret in the river before?" asked Ara picking a long grass stem and putting it in her mouth.

"No, I have put the flax in a pond before. Many people do it, but the smell is awful, and it ruins the pond unless it's fed by a spring. Even then, the pond takes a long time to return to normal. That's why most of us ret on the ground. It takes many weeks longer, but it doesn't harm any water," explained her mother.

Ara was confused. "What would cause the pond water to go bad?"

A soft breeze rippled their kirtles. "It's similar to when I make chamomile tea. When I steep the dry flowers in hot water, it flavors and colors the water as it softens the petals. You can smell the tea, too. Retting in water does the same thing. The dry flax softens so we can get to the fibers. While it is softening, it gives off color and a bad smell."

Ara nodded in understanding. "But won't the flax ruin the water in the river?"

"I don't think so," replied her mother. "The water is constantly flowing, so it should carry any leeching from the flax away."

As promised, the rocks were lying on the ground on the bank. Amelie tied one end of the rope to a wagon wheel and the other around her middle. She looked around. No one was in sight, so she took off her shoes and hiked up her kirtle and smock, tucking them into the rope at her waist.

"Mama, what are you doing?" Ara was shocked. She had never seen her mother so immodest outside the house.

"The bottom is slippery and the water is a little fast. If I fall, I can pull on the rope to right myself up." Then she waded in the water with a sheaf of flax in her hand. "Give me a rock."

Ara handed her mother a rock which she positioned atop the bundle. "Give me another." She needed two to secure the flax under the water. "Hand me another bundle and some rocks."

The two of them worked slowly. Jana dropped down to the ground hopping about calling Amelie's name. "I'm fine, Jana," soothed Amelie. She turned to Ara. "He doesn't like this one bit." She paused. "The water's cold." She splashed some water up on the bird. "Do you want a bath?"

Jana croaked, "Stop!" and flew to a nearby branch, shaking his feathers.

"Brrrr. Let's finish this up." It took an hour to complete the task. Using the rope, Amelie began pulling herself out of the water. She slipped and went down on one knee. "Oh!" she exclaimed.

Jana quawed and flew into Amelie's hair. She laughed, getting up quickly. "He's trying to pull me out of the water."

"Are you all right?" gasped Ara, taking her mother's extended hand and pulling her up.

Amelie looked down at her stockings. "I'm fine. My stockings are green from the river bottom, though. That's the worst of it." She picked Jana up from the ground. "You are my hero," she said and gave him a kiss on the head.

Three days later, Ara and her mother were planting turnips in the garden in the front of the house and tending to weeds. They were nearly finished when Ara's cousin Freida stopped by.

"Good morning, Aunt Amelie. Good morning, Ara. My mother said I could show you my new doll."

Ara jumped up to look at it, wiping her hands on her apron. "Oh, Frieda, she is beautiful." The doll had a smooth wooden head with a cleverly painted face. Her clothing was made from fabric scraps.

She carefully examined the toy and gave it a hug before returning the doll to her cousin. "Your mother is quite handy with her sewing. What did you name her?"

Freida's dimples showed when she smiled. "I'm calling her Ursula."

Ara suppressed a giggle. She didn't remind her cousin that it was the name of one of her goats. "It's a lovely name," she said, rubbing the arm of her cousin.

Amelie leaned against her shovel. "This is a good time to take a little break. Ara, get your dolly and play with Frieda for a bit. I'm going to the river to check on the flax."

"So soon? We just put it in the river a few days ago," remarked Ara.

"It's hard to say when it will be ready. Usually it only takes about a week to ret in water, but the crop can be ruined if it is left too long. I'll check it early every morning from now on. Now go play. It won't take me long to get there and back."

She began striding to the river, but called back to Ara, "There are some wild berries on the hutch. You two can eat some of them...but not too many."

Several days later Ara woke up late. She didn't hear any pecking at her window. She opened her shutters and called for Jana. "Naughty bird," she scolded. "Where are you? You forgot to wake me."

She got dressed, calling to her mother as she walked downstairs. "Mama, Jana isn't here." There was a loud silence in the room. Her stomach became queazy.

As she ran outside, Jana came into sight croaking and swooping. "Amelie! Amelie!" he cried.

"Mama isn't here, Jana." she called to the bird. "Come down here. We'll go find her."

But Jana kept circling and darting, calling Amelie's name. He flew off towards the river. Alarmed, Ara ran after the bird. When she got to the riverbank, she saw that most of the flax had been disturbed and was drifting down the river. Ara looked around but there was no sign of her mother.

Jana squawked and croaked and dove toward the water. That's when Ara saw her mother floating face down further along in the river.

"Mama!" she screamed and jumped into the water. The bottom was slimy and she promptly slipped under. She came up gasping. She waded out until the water was up to her neck before she could reach out and grab her mother's skirt. She towed her towards the bank, falling several times before getting her to the water's edge. Then she turned her face up and pulled her up the bank.

Her mother's eyes were glassy and her body lifeless. A wide gash lay across her forehead to her nose. "Mama, wake up!" Ara shook her mother's body, but there was no response.

Jana flew down next to her. "Amelie! Amelie!" he cried repeatedly, hopping around her head.

Ara jumped up and sprinted to the mill. "Papa! Papa! Papa!" she shouted.

Peter Miller was outside helping a peasant unload sacks of barley when he spotted his daughter. He heard the panic in her voice and ran to her.

"Mama! She was in the water," Ara gasped.

He bolted down the path, fear driving him. Spying his wife on the riverbank, he slid down to her side. He turned her on her stomach and began pressing her back with both hands clenched together. Water spilled from her mouth. Ara stood at the top of the bank shaking with cold and terror. Over and over he pushed, entreating his wife. "Come on, Amelie, wake up!" he repeated. He pushed and begged long after any hope was left.

Peter finally sat back and held his wife's lifeless body in his arms. He closed her eyes and kissed them, and traced her gash with his finger. He buried his head in her neck and sobbed. Ara slipped down to the other side of Amelie, covering her cold hand with her own. It was a long time before her father lifted her mother up and carried her body all the way back to the house. They didn't notice Jana fly off.

CHAPTER 5

Life changed. After the funeral, the village women took turns sending food, but that tapered off quickly. At her aunt's insistence, Ara visited her several times so the woman could help improve her cooking skills. Ara was grateful but quiet. A wan smile occasionally came to her lips, but her eyes remained downturned. She often fidgeted with her mother's ring that the priest had slipped into her hand at the end of her mother's service. She placed it on her third finger where it fit comfortably.

Peter returned to work, staying for longer periods of time. He was shoring up the sagging mill roof, he would say, or repairing the paddle wheel. There was always something to do at the Old Man to keep him from returning to a home without Amelie. His visits to the tavern lasted longer, and he sometimes needed assistance returning home. He was too full of grief to reach out to his daughter, and staring at the empty chair across from him at supper was unbearable.

Ara was alone keeping house and cooking. She kept the garden weeded, the chickens fed, the eggs collected, and cared for the nannies and horse. She no longer touched her toys, and spurned her friends. She did not want to hear them laugh, and she definitely did not want to hear them talk about their mothers.

Her only comfort was Jana. He had flown off the day Amelie died, but returned a week after the funeral. Ara forgave him for not being there. "I didn't want to go, either," she told him. Once back, he didn't fly away after breakfast as he did before. He stayed with her until bedtime and fluttered up to the apple tree to spend the night. In the morning, he tapped on the shutters, just as he had done for years.

One morning, she heard voices in the field. Looking out her window, she saw two women turning the flax over with long sticks. She hurried out to them. "Good morning to you, Ara," spoke one.

"Good morning, Mrs. Weber, Mrs. Becker. What are you doing here?"

"Your mother was a kind woman. She helped improve our spinning many years ago, so we are thanking her now," explained Mrs. Weber. "We've been coming over every week to turn your flax over to keep it retting properly."

Ara fell into their arms, heaving great sobs that had been in her throat for weeks. "I... miss...my...mm... mother."

The women held her and let her cry until her tears ran dry. "Shhh. We know," hushed Mrs. Weber. "We know."

Ara wiped her nose on her apron. "It's not the same without her."

"No," Mrs. Becker shook her head, "It will never be the same. But she raised you to be strong. And she taught you good skills. We will help you get your flax ready. It should be fully retted in a week's time. We'll come back to help you break and scutch it."

"We'll bring our breaks and scutching boards to make the job go faster," promised Mrs. Weber.

"And I will bring bread from the bakery," added Mrs. Becker. "I'll have my husband make us a special loaf to share." She put her arm around Ara's waist. "We'll walk you back to your house. I have a pot of jam you can put away for later."

The week went a little faster for Ara. She was busy harvesting the ripening pears and apples. Some she sliced for drying, spreading them out in trays and putting them in the sun. Others were placed in cold storage along with turnips and parsnips. She brought dough to the village oven. She gave a loaf to her aunt who declared it both crusty and tender. "You have mastered the art of the loaf," she said. For the first time, Ara looked up and smiled.

"Now, my dear," questioned Aunt Clare as she walked her to the door, "have you done any wash yet?" Immediately Ara teared up and shook her head. Her body trembled at the thought of going to the river.

"Tomorrow is my washing day. I will come to your house and we will go to the river together. Take the sheets off the beds. You can wash those, too."

It was hard for Ara to sleep that night. She kept seeing her mother in the water. When Jana woke her up in the morning, her eyes were swollen from crying and her head was pounding. Numbly she donned her kirtle over her smock, stripped both beds, and brought the linens downstairs. She was outside waiting when her aunt pulled up in the wagon. She looked at Ara's bundles. "Do you have all your clothes?" Ara nodded. "Your father's clothes and the bed linens from both beds?"

"Yes, Aunt."

"Your washing bat?"

Ara raised the bat. "Right here."

"Good girl. Put it all in the wagon and climb up." Ara put her bundles in the back of the wagon.

Together they went down to the river. There were several women already down by the jetty. "Good morning, Mrs. Cooper. Good morning, Miss Miller," they called. "This is a fine day, thank goodness." They chatted among themselves. Together they cleaned their belongings, batting them with sticks and placing them on bushes to dry. It was a long and tedious day. Ara stretched her back and shivered from the cold water, grateful that this was an infrequent task.

When they returned to her house, her aunt helped her make up the beds. "You are handling the household well," she said.

"I'm trying." Ara cast her eyes to the floor and twisted her ring.

Aunt Clare lifted the girl's chin. "You're succeeding." She gave her a brisk hug. As she was leaving, she spoke again. "I'll pick you up tomorrow for church," and swiftly closed the door behind her before Ara could answer.

Ara set out goat cheese and eggs for supper. Her father came home dusty with grain. She had learned to keep her distance from him now. He grunted a greeting and sat at the table without washing up. She placed a cup of cider in front of him. "I'll have ale," he muttered.

"Sorry, Papa," she said and withdrew the cup and poured him some ale. The two of them ate in silence, he in his chair and she on the bench. He had moved Amelie's chair into the weaving room so he didn't have to look at it standing empty across from him.

When Peter was finished, he pushed away from the table. Wordlessly, he walked out the door. Ara's eyes welled. She knew he was grieving, but so was she. She wished they could comfort each other. Sighing, she cleaned up the kitchen and fell exhausted into bed. She was asleep as soon as she closed her eyes.

Ara had just enough time to feed the animals and get dressed before the Cooper family arrived. Uncle Jasper, smelling slightly of the oak staves he shaped and formed into barrels, lifted her into the back of the wagon. Frieda and her brother Mannus moved over to make room for her in the back. Frieda took her hand and Ara held it tightly. It was the first time she was returning to mass since her mother's death. Her father was angry with God and was sleeping off a long night at the tavern.

Mannus bowed slightly to Ara but otherwise acted indifferently towards her. He kept a peripheral look on her, though. His cousin was growing into a beauty. It was hard to ignore her thick, dark hair even under her coif, and her deep blue eyes had long captivated him. She was thinner than Frieda, but he remembered her as strong and wiry. Today was the first day something inside him stirred. Mannus was apprenticing at his father's cooper shop. He would take over it someday, and at sixteen, was beginning to consider the village girls as wives. Ara would make a good mate.

Both Aunt Clare and Freida wrapped their arms around Ara's waist as they walked into the church. They could feel the hesitation in her step. She was angry with God, too. Mr. Kaufmann's stomach began churning when she walked in. He had been to mass every day since Amelie's death and lighted countless candles. His clothes hung on him and his face sagged. Guilt wracked his thoughts.

The mass soothed her. The droning Latin language of the Catholic Church was familiar to her, as were the faces in the congregation. She twisted the golden wheat ring on her finger and prayed for mother's soul, although she knew it could be nowhere but in heaven.

After mass her friends surrounded her. Ara had been missed. They greeted her warmly and invited her to visit. She took a deep breath. *I must go on,* she thought. *Mama would be disappointed in me if I don't carry on. It is just what she did when she lost her family when she was young.*

The clattering of a wagon outside the door told Ara that Mrs. Becker and Mrs. Weber were there with the breaks and scutching boards. The day was sunny and dry, a perfect day for the task at hand. "We'll head into the field while you get your equipment, too."

Ara ran to the barn. The scutching board and accompanying knife were light enough to carry, but she needed help carrying the break. The waist high wooden piece of equipment stood on splayed legs with three boards spaced apart from one another across the top. Above those was a wooden blade that could be raised and lowered.

When everything was in place, Mrs. Becker instructed, "Mrs. Weber and I will break the stalks to free the fiber. That will get rid of most of the useless boon, but not all of it. We'll hand it off to you, and you can scutch it clean of the rest. First, though, you can start breaking the fibers with us until we have enough for you to begin scutching. Let us show you how to do it."

Both women took a handful of flax stalks by the root end and raised the blade. They lay the flax across the three boards and forcefully lowered the blade over the stalks moving them backwards towards the top of the plant. They repeated the motion several times until most of the boon fell off.

"Now you try it," Mrs. Becker urged.

Dutifully Ara mimicked their actions. The women were being so kind and patient, she was loathe to tell them she had been doing this job for the past couple of years. What was different this time, however, was that she had grown several inches. Her leverage was better as well as her strength.

"Good job," remarked Mrs. Weber. "Let's get busy." Together they worked and talked. The women were clever in their conversation. What seemed to be idle small talk to Ara were really cooking, gardening, and household cleaning hints. Amelie must be smiling down on them and giving invisible hugs.

Without instruction, Ara picked up the scutching board and blade and began scraping the last of the boon from the flax. The fibers were getting smoother. When all the breaking had been done, the two women joined her in scutching. It was an altogether pleasant early autumn afternoon. The sun was beginning its downward descent when they finished.

Ara faced both women. "You have been generous with your time and help." She spread her arms. "I could not have finished this job without you."

"We are glad to help you. We are doing this as much for your mother as for you," said Mrs. Becker, "and it's our Christian duty to be of service." She continued, "We will come next week and help you hackle the fibers."

"Thank you, but I can do that. My mother taught me. Now that this job is done, I can hackle a bit at a time. I'll put the flax in the house and work on it when I'm able." She didn't say that she had plenty of lonely time to fill with her mother buried and her father away each night.

"All right. We'll help you put your tools away." Together the three of them carried Ara's equipment to the barn. Then they returned to get the women's tools and put them in the wagon.

"Mercy me," exclaimed Mrs. Becker when both women were seated. "I promised to bring a special bread for us to share, and I completely forgot." She lifted a loaf from her basket at her feet. "Here, you take it." She bent down and handed it to Ara. "It has seeds and berries in it. Have it at supper tonight."

"You are very generous." Ara embraced it. "I am sure to enjoy it." She waved as they drove off, and only when they were far enough away did Jana come flying down from his perch. She had been aware of him watching closely all day.

Together they went into the house and she broke off a piece of bread for him. He took it in his beak and fluttered up to the hutch. No one but her family knew of him. He would have been too difficult to explain.

She unwrapped some cheese and took a pear from the table. That and the bread would be her dinner tonight. She knew she had to begin cooking more regularly for her father's sake. He never complained about supper, though, because he didn't care. He didn't care much about anything these days.

I have to get out of the house, she thought to herself in the morning. The nightly dreams of her mother were vivid, and to wake up with no sound of her bustling around downstairs added to her heartache. Thank goodness for Jana. He had been her comfort. In the first weeks after Amelie's death, he didn't leave Ara's side. She paused to think about that. *He needed me just as much as I needed him,* she mused.

Since the beginning of the week, though, Jana had been leaving her bedside at night returning to his usual perch until morning. It was his cue for her to return, as much as she could, to her old routine. *There is no old routine,* she thought ruefully, *but I will make my life happy once more. I must.*

She thought of her father. His sadness was palpable. Having a happy, loving marriage has a high cost when it ends. Ara was awake before him every morning. "You must eat," she entreated him. "Mama would not want you to go off without a full stomach."

This morning he sat down to break his fast. Lord Belstrum had sent tiny boxes of spices as a mourning gift, and she had put a little cinnamon in his porridge. "This tastes different," he remarked. It was the first time he had spoken to her in the morning in a month.

"I put a bit of spice in the meal," she said, "as a treat. I hope you like it."

Her father grunted and finished it wordlessly. He arose from the table and held her close. "You are a good daughter," he said at last, letting her go. He sighed, put on his cap and waistcoat, and left.

A gentle, swishing breeze rode through the trees as Ara strolled the short way to the village. The warm sun high in the sky felt good on her face, but it had been crisp the last few nights. Persimmon and yellow hues were edging the leaves. She had tied her hair back with a ribbon, but it loosened, so she stopped to refasten it. The scent of grapes being pressed wafted from the vineyards. Amber wines would be ready soon.

"Good afternoon, Mr. Metzger," Ara greeted the butcher when she entered his shop.

His face brightened when he saw her. The stocky man put down his cleaver and rubbed his hands clean. "Hello there, Miss Miller. What brings you here this fine afternoon?"

"I am going to make my father a roast tomorrow. What do you recommend?"

"I have some fine hams. Let me get one for you." He brought her a small ham. "This should do fine. Look, I've left fat on this one. Salt half of it to keep it for other meals. If you take some strips of the meat and fat, you can fry it up in your spider and serve it with eggs and bread." He paused. "Wait, I will cut some up for you myself."

Ara waited patiently for the man to finish the task. "Here you go. This will be a treat for your father."

"Thank you, Mr. Metzger," Ara smiled. She handed the butcher a few coins. "Have a good day,"

Mr. Kaufmann caught sight of her as she was walking to see Mrs. Becker at the bakery. He hurried out to greet her. "Miss Miller, how fine it is to see you out and about."

Ara noticed how thin and haggard his face had become. "Good day to you, Sir."

"I was hoping to see you. Your mother," tears welling in his eyes, "was such a good woman."

Ara could do nothing more than stand erect; the lump in her throat preventing her from speaking.

"She brought me the finest linen in all the village. Everyone agrees that hers was the best."

Ara remained mute. It was true. She had seen it with her own eyes, felt it with her own hands. It was softer, whiter, and more delicate than any other. Plus, her dyed threads were more vibrant than any other.

"I would like to buy your linen and threads, just as I have purchased your mother's."

Her eyebrows raised. "But you have not seen my work. It does not compare to my mother's."

"I have every confidence that it will one day, and I will have secured you in the meantime." He reached out to put his hand on her arm, but quickly changed his mind.

"Why, thank you, Mr. Kaufmann. I will be pleased to bring my work to you." Her face lit up. She was now a working woman.

CHAPTER 6

Ara worked steadily on making her linen threads as thin as possible. If she made them too delicate, they would break, so finding the point where they were fine yet strong was her goal. It took her four years to perfect her threads, and, at last, she was satisfied.

Mr. Kaufmann bent over the fabric with a magnifying glass. The threads were nearly as fine as spider silk. He pulled in all directions. It was strong and soft and supple. He leaned back in his chair and raised his eyes to Ara. "You have surpassed your mother. I have never seen such exquisite work. Never."

The serious young woman standing in front of him looked much different than the girl he struck a deal with years ago. The gleam was gone from her eyes. Her face had lost its roundedness of youth. A maturity had set in her cheeks and the shape of her chin. She stood nearly as tall as he, well, as tall as he used to be. Then she smiled and her eyes lit up once more. *I feared her joy was gone forever,* he thought.

"Spinning has become my passion," said Ara, "almost a compulsion. It brings me serenity and conjures up the most wonderful memories of my mother. She is with me when I spin."

"Her hands must be guiding you. She's spinning through you."

"Why, yes, I believe so," agreed Ara.

He tottered over to the cash box. He was rail thin now and stooped. Asking Mrs. Miller to ret in the river had cast a guilt over him as heavy as a mill stone. For the first year after her death, he wore a hair shirt as penance, until the priest ordered him to remove it. "You will suffer with this guilt for the rest of your life. You must find another way to atone your sin."

"Well, now, to the matter of payment." He lifted his money box from beneath the wooden counter, and handed her several coins. "This is more than in the past because the fair is soon. I will sell it then. People will be coming from different villages. Some noble men and women will be here, too. One of them will pay a dear price for it."

Ara accepted the payment and thanked him, tucking the coins in a bag at her waist. She trusted him because her mother did. She had no way of knowing that he paid her twice the worth of the cloth.

"When will you have more?"

"Soon. I am nearly finished weaving some fabric for myself. Then I will begin again for you." She adjusted her coif on her head. "I will see you at service on Sunday. Goodbye, Mr. Kaufmann."

"Goodbye, Miss Miller. Give my regards to your father."

"Perhaps you will see him at the tavern tonight." She reminded him of her father's frequent visits there.

"Yes, yes," he said distractedly, "perhaps."

The praise from Mr. Kaufmann lightened her step. Acorns cracked under her feet as she left the village, and she tilted her head up to the rays of the sun. When she was a child, she rarely went to the mill. "Your papa is very busy," her mother would say. Now she stopped in several times a week. Today she looked forward to telling him her good news.

"Hello, Papa," she greeted him. Three workers were busy milling the new grains as her father stood back and watched. Peter turned when he heard his name. "Ara, my daughter, you have come to visit." Her happiness faded when she saw her father's drooping yellow eyes. His face was sallow and swollen from drink.

"I have stopped in to see how you are getting on." She forced a smile to her lips.

"We are very busy here. I just unloaded all those sacks there," he pointed to the pile in the corner. "We're expecting more today."

"Good," she responded. Ara knew he was lying, but she wasn't sure if he knew it. He was too unsteady on his feet to work today. The younger men had done it for him. She called to Sig. "Make sure he gets home safely, will you?" Sig was her father's first employee. She knew she could count on him.

"Sure. I'll walk him home when we're done here," he answered. He stopped filling a sack, put down his scoop and strode over to her. "Can I have a moment of your time, though?" They walked out of the mill together. He hesitated before he began. "Your father's drinking is getting worse. Some of the peasants are complaining about the fantastical stories he's telling them."

Ara pressed her lips together. "What kind of stories?"

"He tells one about killing a boar with his bare hands, and another about a giant who threw him to the moon. He said he had to swim in the air to make it back to Earth. Your father takes up their time and they see he's not doing his work. The men here see it, too. They no longer trust him to handle the sacks, let alone the milling stones. His drinking interferes with his work as well as his memory."

She sighed heavily and pinched her eyes with her thumb and forefinger. There was a time when Ara entreated her father to stop drinking. "Mama would hate to see you like this," she had cried. Even her Aunt Clare and Uncle Jasper's imploring failed. He had always been a storyteller, but now his drinking was making him confuse reality and fantasy.

"I will speak with him," Ara promised Sig, and slowly walked home. The good news from Mr. Kaufmann faded. When she arrived at her cottage, she climbed the stairs to her room. It was small and spare. Against one wall was a bed made of slats with rope strung across. Atop it rested a woolen mattress with a quilt neatly folded at the bottom. Ara went directly to the oaken chest on the other side of the room. When she opened it, the smell of lavender and mugwort filled her nostrils. She reached through her clothes and fumbled with a woolen sack. She could feel the heft of the coins inside. She hated the thought of hiding them from her father, but these were her savings in case...in case.... Ara tried not to finish her thought. In case he lost his job? In case he died?

She needed to be prepared for an "in case." The cottage belonged to the miller, but one day he might not be the miller. Where would she go? She was of an age when she should begin to think about marriage, but who would marry her? What would she have to show for a dowery? Her father drank most of his earnings. This bag of coins was all she had. She dropped her new coins in, tied the sack, and slipped it back under her clothes.

Peter ate his supper silently, unaware of his food spilling onto his shirt and the table. He left soon after to go to the tavern. Ara shook her head and cleaned up before she settled in to spin. She sang softly to herself, bending every now and then to wet her fingers as the fibers spun into fine thread. It was late evening before she headed to bed.

Ara bolted upright when she heard banging on the door. "Ara, it's Uncle Jasper. Let me in!" She rushed down the stairs and opened the door. Uncle Jasper had his arms around her father, and half carried, half dragged him in the house. "Mr. Becker found him lying on the ground halfway to the house," he said after he lowered Peter into the chair. "He didn't want to frighten you so late at night, so he brought him to me. Look, his face is bleeding."

She tended to the scrapes on her father's face. "Papa, Papa, are you all right?"

"I'm fine," he slurred. "Get me to bed."

Ara and her uncle helped him upstairs and laid him across his bed. Then they went downstairs to talk. "This is the third time this month he's needed help getting home," Ara sighed. She put her head in her hands. "He's going to drink himself to death."

"I knew he was a heavy drinker, but I didn't know he was this bad."

Ara told him how often her father stumbled drunk back into the cottage. Twice recently he was too sick to make it to work the next day, and arriving at the mill late was becoming a habit. "I don't know how much longer it'll be before he gets let go from the mill."

Jasper began pacing wordlessly. Finally he sat down and leaned forward. "It's time you came to live with Aunt Clare and me. It's not right for you to live with such a drunken father."

She shook her head. "No, I couldn't. He's a sick man who mourns my mother still. He will die if I go."

"I'll talk with Aunt Clare...and I'll have myself a long talk with your father. This has to stop." Jasper spoke through clenched teeth.

Ara spoke ruefully. "Truly, my father has only gone through the motions of living since my mother died. I can see that he only hangs on to this life because I am here, even though he is silent whenever he is home. I have accepted that drink will kill him," she paused, "and maybe that will be a blessing to him, to be reunited with my mother sooner rather than later." She walked her uncle to the door. "When he dies, I will come live with you, but I'll remain here for now."

The next morning Ara tried waking her father to no avail. Jana waited for her on the upstairs railing. "I'm afraid he won't be going into work today," she said to the bird. "I have some fish for you on the hutch. Go eat while I go to the mill to let them know."

Jana watched as she spent much of the morning hackling and combing flax. She used a series of hackles, running handfuls of flax through the teeth making the flax finer and finer. Finally, she combed them, separating the long strands from the short. Ara went to check on her father. He was snoring, so she left him alone.

Grabbing her straw hat and a basket, she went out to the garden to find what she could gather. It was a good task to shake the webs of worry from her mind. She picked some lettuce and beans, parsnips and cabbage. She set out the beans to dry on a wooden board, and sliced a couple of parsnips and cabbage to boil with the lamb she was making for supper.

She found peace working in the garden. It was a mindless task to weed. She grabbed the hoe and hummed a tune her mother had taught her. The fresh air invigorated her, making her mind lighter. Jana stayed near her in the garden. He helped by searching out and eating the insects that were munching on the leaves. "Stay away from the spiders," Ara cautioned him. "They are our friends in the the garden."

Peter awoke in the evening. Ara heard him moving and rushed upstairs to help him. The smell in the room made her gag. He had vomited onto the floor and the bed was soaked with urine. She brought him clean clothes and washed him as best as she could before she brought him some water to drink. Her father was barely coherent.

Using shuffling steps, she steered him to her room and put him in her own bed. "Come on, Papa. Here, lie down." Wordlessly, he obeyed her and fell back to sleep. She spent the rest of the evening cleaning his room. That night as she dressed for bed, she touched her necklace and stared at her ring, spinning it around with her thumb. *Papa might be with you soon*, she silently addressed her mother. She tiptoed down the stairs and made a nest with some blankets before falling into a restless sleep.

When she awoke, Ara found her father sitting at the table. "How are you feeling?" she asked.

"Better," he mumbled. She looked him over. His eyes were as yellow as was his skin, but he appeared more alert.

"I'm going to get ready for the Coopers. They'll be by to pick me up for church soon. I'll get you some breakfast before I go."

The Cooper family came by to collect her for church each Sunday. Ara looked forward to it, not so much for the service, but for the socializing that followed. Although her cousin Mannus still thought her a possibility as a wife, he began to notice other young women in the village, as well. Ara, for her part, never considered him for a husband. Her disposition had grown serious over the years and he was childish still.

There was a time after mass when the girls would gather in one circle and the boys in another, but now they joined together, the young women and men, each silently assessing others as mates. Ara was attracted to the eldest Becker son. He was working in his family's bakery and would run the shop one day. At least, thought Ara, I would never go hungry if we married. He was pleasing to look at and well groomed.

He, in turn, was attentive to her. She was a mature young woman, but he wished she smiled more. His mother encouraged a match. "Ara is hard working and has a pleasant disposition. She will stay by your side and be honorable to you. She knows all the household tasks and will make extra money by spinning and weaving."

There was great excitement among all the people gathering outside the church. The fair was to be held for two days this week, and merchants were coming from all over Europe. All sorts of spices, cheeses, meats, and wine would be sold. For the peasants, it was a break from their every day life, and for the noble class, it was an opportunity to buy merchandise from exotic locales. Sellers had been busy setting up stalls all week, including the local merchants who were not allowed to open up their stores during the fair.

There would be entertainment, too, including plays, magicians, acrobats, and jugglers. There was a rumor that there would even be a dancing bear. Several contests would be held, including some for children who could win prizes.

Ara and her friends were in their circle talking about the fair. "I am hoping to buy a piece of lace," said Freida. "It would make a pretty collar on my gown."

Several of the other young women agreed. "I would like some, too, for my sleeves," remarked another.

There were many hopes and wishes. "Maybe I will purchase cinnamon and cloves," "I want to buy a foreign cheese. I am bored with the ones here." "A delicious red wine." "I want to see the dancing bear."

Ara felt a hand on her elbow. When she turned, she faced Klaus Becker. Her face lit up. "Are you going to the fair, Ara?" he asked.

They stepped away from the group. "Yes, I will go with my aunt and uncle and cousins. Will you be going, as well?"

Klaus laughed. "I believe the whole of the village is going. Your uncle has asked me to join them for the first day. I hope that pleases you."

Ara could feel the heat on her cheeks. "Yes, that pleases me. I hope it is not an inconvenience to you."

"Not at all. I am quite happy that arrangement has been made." He bowed. "I look forward to seeing you on Wednesday."

On the ride home, Aunt Clare said, "By the way, I have asked Frederick Weber and Klaus Becker to join us at the fair. Mannus, you will be going with the Ziegler family." Ara and her cousins eyed each other and grinned. It would be a good fair.

CHAPTER 7

Ara rose early the morning of the fair. Jana sat with her as she ate her porridge. She sprinkled some nuts into it, saving some for her bird. "Here you go, my friend." He ate one from her hand and she set the others on the table. "Come with me while I feed the animals."

She hurried out to the barn. Jana settled atop the goat stall. The nannies looked up at her and bleated. Ursula and Gertie each had two kids suckling at their teats. She fed all the animals and hurried inside to wash and change.

The kirtle Ara selected was a new one she had made from her linen. Much care had gone into making it. She had beaten the madder root to make the red dye. The red ribbon she wove through her braided hair matched her kirtle.

Ara stood in the doorway of her father's bedroom. His back was to her as he snored loudly through his dreams. There was no reason to wake him this morning since everything had been shut down for the fair. She turned away, rubbed her necklace secreted under her smock, a ritual she continued since her mother's death, and scurried down the stairs.

She put a pear and two hardboiled eggs on a plate on the table for him. Then she cut two slices of bread, buttered them, and covered the meal with a cloth. She was outside and waiting for the Coopers when they came to collect her. Klaus and Frederick strode up with them.

A cloudless sky allowed the sun to show bright and clear. An early rain had left traces of ozone in the air. "It's a glorious day, so we decided to walk," announced Aunt Clare. She and Uncle Jasper led the way, and Ara and Freida paired off behind with the young men.

Klaus cleared his throat. "You look lovely today."

"I...I...thank you," she stammered, feeling the warmth of a blush starting at her neck. "You look very handsome." And he did. He was nearly a head taller than Ara with a bush of brown hair tied into a knot on the top of his head. His sinewy arms and trim waist formed a pleasing figure.

The noise of the fair greeted them as soon as they passed the walls of the village. Throngs of people filled the streets with more streaming in. People were laughing and shouting to each other. Ara's ears were filled with strange languages and loud music. Unfamiliar fragrances floated through the air. It was fun already.

Frieda, Ara, and their escorts made plans to meet the adults later in the afternoon, and off they went in search of adventure. The couples first made their way to the acrobats.

They applauded and whooped at them as they twirled in the air and flipped onto one another's shoulders.

Next they watched a puppet show. It was a biblical tale about the prodigal son performed in French. Even though the language was strange, the story was familiar. As they walked around, they stopped at stalls to admire trinkets and smell perfumed oils. They were interested in everything. Minstrels strolled around singing songs.

"I believe there is an archery competition at the far end of the village," said Frieda. "Let's go see it." As they strolled down the street, rich aromas of unfamiliar foods swirling through the air attracted them to the comestibles booths. They were tempted by the smells of melting cheeses and bubbling stews, but the savory fragrances from the Florentine booth brought them to immediate agreement.

They each purchased walking meals of crusty bread filled with roasted sausage and onions. "This sausage is different from ours," remarked Klaus.

"It's the spices that are different," Frieda noted. "I definitely taste garlic in it. Your turn," she directed at Ara.

Ara took a bite and sucked on the meat. "Hmm, there's fennel in it. Definitely fennel...and paprika." She turned to Frederick.

"I really can't say which spices are in here. I only know that this is the best thing I've ever eaten in my life," he rolled his eyes with pleasure.

When they arrived at the archery competition, Mannus and some of their friends had already taken their positions to shoot. "Hurry up. Get in line," Ara encouraged the young men. Klaus and Frederick each paid a coin to compete. They scored well, but not enough to earn a prize.

"We better keep the peace with all the other kingdoms," laughed Klaus, "because we would not fare well protecting ourselves."

"Except for Mannus," interjected Freida. "He had three bullseyes."

They came to a section of the fair where fabrics were sold. There were wondrous silks from the Far East in strong hues of reds and blues. The wools from Britannia had patterns of stripes and herringbone and plaids. Ara took her time running her hands over the cloths, feeling the textures, and making a mental note to try some of the designs when she next loomed her threads.

As they were wandering through the maze of stalls, she heard her name being shouted. She looked around and saw Mr. Kaufmann beckoning from near his store where a table for his wares had been set up. "Miss Miller!" He called her over.

"Good day, Mr. Kaufmann," Ara greeted him gaily, glancing at his booth. "I see you have sold nearly all of your goods."

"Yes, it has been a lucrative day for me, but I have exciting news for you!" He could not keep the grin from his face. "I told you I would get a good price for your fabric. The king's treasurer was here and he purchased it! He said it was the finest example of linen work he had ever seen, and he wanted to know who made it. I told him Ara, the miller's daughter. The lord said he would show it to the king himself."

Ara's hands went to her mouth and then to her cheeks. "I am so flattered," she breathed. "The king will see my work!"

Frieda beamed along with Ara, embracing her. "Congratulations, Ara. Your hard work has been recognized. I hope you are proud of yourself."

"This is a good day for you." Mr. Kaufmann smiled. "Now go on and enjoy the rest of the festival."

Ara spent the rest of the day in high spirits. Every song she heard was beautiful. Every aroma was magnificent. To make the day complete, the group even saw the dancing bear. Ara laughed and clapped the loudest.

Night had set in by the time they met up with Mr. and Mrs. Cooper. Ara was surprised and pleased to see her father with them. "We went back to the house and got him out of bed. He should enjoy the fair, too," said her uncle. Peter looked better than he had in days. Frieda was animated as she told them Ara's good news. Her aunt's eyes pricked. *Ara has needed something exciting and rewarding,* she thought. She clasped her niece and kissed her forehead.

Ara could not keep a smile from her lips. This was the best day of her life. She had fun at the fair, enjoyed the company of Klaus, and learned that the king would see her handiwork.

With a nod from her aunt, Klaus walked her home. "I enjoyed the day with you, Ara."

"I did, too," she replied.

His foot scraped the ground. Suddenly he was shy. "If it is acceptable to you, I would like to see you again."

"I would like that."

"Perhaps we can go for a stroll after mass on Sunday?"

"That would be nice, indeed."

Klaus bowed. "Goodnight then, Ara."

"Goodnight, Klaus." She spun around and went inside, running up the stairs to her room. "Jana! Jana!" she called from the window. The bird left his perch and flew to the sill.

"Ara," he said. "Pretty Ara."

"The king is going to see my linen," she enthused. "Imagine that!"

Jana hopped along the base of the window. "Pretty Ara," he repeated and flew back to the tree.

CHAPTER 8

Peter was putting his second leg into his hose when he heard the clatter of hooves. He finished dressing as quickly as he could. By the time he reached the bottom of the staircase, someone was knocking loudly on the door. Swinging it open, he stood face to face with a man wearing aa richly embroidered black velvet doublet and fulled woolen breeches.

"Are you the miller?" the man inquired. He was holding the reins of the tallest steed Peter had ever seen. Braided into its mane were shimmery bangles that tinkled when the horse shook its head. Silver stirrups hung from the carved leather saddle.

"That I am, Peter Miller," he responded. "Can I help you, Sir?"

The gentleman reached out to grasp Peter's hand. His cheery voice matched his open smile. "A pleasant morning to you. I am Lord Huber. I have been visiting your good Lord Belstrum. Lady Belstrum showed me the most splendid linen that was purchased from Mr. Kauffman. I went to his booth at the festival and bought what he had. He told me your daughter spun and wove it and that she might have more at home. I would like to purchase all she has. It is as fine a cloth that I ever saw made from flax."

Peter shifted his weight. "She learned the skill from her mother, God rest her soul. She was the best around."

"She taught your daughter well. I have never seen such thin strands of thread gotten from linen.

"Yes, yes," bragged Peter. He straightened out his belt and stood a little taller. "Her mother taught her a trick or two on the spinning wheel." He lowered his voice to a whisper. "She even taught her to spin straw into gold."

Lord Huber's eyes widened. "You are jesting, Sir."

"No, I am not." The miller was full of himself now. "She would deny it, but it is true."

"That is too hard to believe. I would need proof of such a thing."

Peter leaned in. "I am but a poor miller, yet my daughter wears a ring made of gold. She made it out of wheat straw."

Lord Huber was apprehensive. "I must see it to believe it. Where is she?"

The miller shrugged. "She may be in the field. I will go check." He walked around the back of the cottage and saw Ara tilling the flax plot, preparing it for a crop of oats. Jana was on the ground next to her.

"Ara!" he called. She raised her head and swiveled to looked at him. "Come here!" He waved her in. "Someone wants to meet you. Quickly now."

She lay down the hoe and hurried back to the house. Jana flew up to the housetop. "Someone is here?" she asked, smoothing her hair and readjusting her coif.

She walked to the front of the cottage with her father and stopped when she saw the glossy chestnut horse. She took a sharp inhale of air. It was the grandest horse she'd ever seen. Her gaze turned to the man standing nearby. She guessed by his opulent attire that he was the man who purchased her cloth. Her heart began thrumming.

Lord Huber walked over to Ara and held out his hands palm up. Unsure of what to do, Ara put her hands in his and curtseyed awkwardly. He looked down at her hands and spied the wheat shaped ring.

So it is true! The ring looks like a golden stalk of wheat twisted around her finger A strange form of alchemy, indeed, thought the nobleman. If he hired her as his servant, he could be richer than the king. He quickly rethought that idea. *If the king finds out that I had such a girl, I will be nothing but a head on a spike. I am better off getting a reward from the king and keeping myself in one piece.*

He bowed and kept himself outwardly calm. "You are the maker of the cloth I purchased yesterday?" he inquired.

"I am," she answered.

"The king will want to meet someone who makes such beautiful cloth. I will take you to him."

Ara took a step back and looked at her father. "Papa, am I to go? I cannot travel alone with a man."

"Of course your father will join you," Lord Huber assured her. "Both of you will accompany me to to meet King Richard. I have two servants who will bring my wagon here shortly."

Peter nudged closer to the visitor. "How long will we be gone?"

"Let us say three days only. If we leave soon, we will be at the Lundgrin Castle tonight. The king will see you in the morrow, and I will have someone escort you back the following day," replied the Lord. "It is a huge honor," he added turning to Ara. "Get your best dress to wear to meet the king. I have plenty of food for the trip."

She and Peter went into the house to pack. She folded her red kirtle into a sack. Before she left her room, she stretched out her window to call her bird. "Jana, come here."

The bird flew down to her from the rooftop. "Stay near me on this journey. Understand?"

The black bird bobbed his head. "Stay near," he repeated and flew off.

By the time she returned outside, a young couple was driving a wagon down the path from the village. "This is Mr. and Mrs. Knecht," Lord Huber introduced them when they reached the house.

The miller and the male servant shook hands. Ara and the woman nodded a greeting. Ara was both frightened and excited. She clasped her hands in front of her to keep them from shaking. She had never slept away from her cottage before, not even at her aunt's home just a few houses beyond hers. And to meet the king!

"You can ride in the back of the wagon." The woman indicated with her head. She helped Ara and her father get settled among the newly purchased wares from the festival and then climbed onto the seat next to her husband.

Lord Huber mounted his horse, and with a salute, their trek began. Jana soared above.

Huber told Ara and Peter to prepare for a journey that would last until nightfall. They saw many travelers on the road. Some were heading to the feast while others were returning from it. Several of them waved as the wagon lumbered past. Peter, in good spirits, waved back, calling out to people he knew.

Ara had never seen another village, even though the closest one from Belstrumburg was only an hour's ride away. The first one she saw looked similar to hers with a wall encircling it, the mill at the bank of the river, and the large manor house at the top of a hill. As they traveled on the clearly marked road, her view changed from meadow to farm fields to village to forest and back to meadow. They passed other villages of various sizes with manor houses overlooking them. Most of the manor houses were surrounded by wooden walls, but one had tall stone walls with a moat surrounding it. She kept her eyes toward the sky to look for Jana. He appeared high in the air, circling occasionally. This gave her comfort.

Lord Huber alternately walked his horse next to Ara or pranced a little ahead of the wagon. He needed to keep near the prize he was bringing the king. He attempted a conversation but she was unaccustomed to speaking with strange men and was very shy. At first Peter was talkative, but became quieter as the day continued. She could tell he was beginning to feel ill.

The sun set leaving pink and purple blooms hovering above. The moon was brightening in the sky while the Roman and Greek constellations began twinkling their presence. Peter fell deep into a fever sleep. After riding on ahead, Lord Huber returned to the wagon. "Ara, we are nearly arrived. Look."

She had ridden the entire way facing the rear of the wagon. Now she pivoted around and sat up on her knees. Ahead of her loomed Lundgrin Castle. It was the grandest set of buildings she had ever seen, dwarfing Lord Belstrum's manor house. The stone walls traveled to large round towers on the corners and a metal grate that was raised to allow entrance to the courtyard.

As they rode up to the iron portcullis, Ara could make out gardens on three sides and forests beyond them. She strained to see Jana circling above. She roused her father to let him know they had arrived.

They came to a stop inside the courtyard and Mr. Knecht helped her from the wagon. Peter struggled down. Ara straightened her kirtle, and Lord Huber led them inside to the grand hall. Her eyes widened as she looked around. The wooden ceiling arched high above her in a room that could hold her cottage four times over. Geometric shapes were painted between the curved beams, and tall leaded glass windows lined both sides of the room. She circled around to catch sight of it all. It was three times as long as it was wide. Fireplaces at each end were large enough for her to step inside.

Lord Huber excused himself and left them standing in the hall with Mr. Knecht. Ara stood mute supporting her father for half an hour until he returned. "Please, Lord, my father needs a bed. He is not well."

"Certainly, Miss Miller. Mr. Knecht will take your father to his room, and I will escort you to yours." He picked up her small bag, grabbed an oil lamp, and together they took the stairs and strode down a narrow passage to a small bed chamber. A high bed covered in silk rested along one wall and a small mahogany chest with a basin of water stood next to it. Across the room was a table and stool. A single open window let starlight fall into the room.

"A guard will sleep outside your room tonight. If you need anything, just knock on your door and he will answer."

"I would like to check on my father," said Ara.

"Do not worry. I will call for the physician and he will tend to him. He will be well taken care of," he assured her.

Mrs. Knecht appeared at the doorway with a tray of pottage, bread and mead. "I thought you must be hungry after the long trip," she said as she entered and set it down on the table. "Also," she lifted the skirt of the bed to show a chamber pot, "this will come in handy for you."

For the first time, Ara allowed a smile to come to her lips. "I am most grateful to you, Mrs. Knecht."

"You are all set for the night then," said the Lord. "We will take our leave." He placed the oil lamp on the chest, and with a sharp bow, he shut the door leaving Ara alone.

She dashed to the window and called repeatedly for Jana. After a few minutes, the raven found his way to her and flew in. "Good, Jana," she whispered. She broke a piece of bread to give to him and dunked another into the hot, herbal soup. She managed to eat half the meal but was too anxious about meeting the king for anything more. She sat on the bed and stroked Jana's wings to calm herself. Exhaustion eventually overtook her. She readied herself for bed and climbed under the covers. It didn't take long for sleep to come. Jana flew to the windowsill, sat for a few moments, and winged off.

She awoke to the knocking at the door. "It is Greta Knecht. I've come with your breakfast." Ara scrambled out of bed, wiping the sand from her eyes. She opened the door to a warm, inviting face.

"Thank you, Mrs. Knecht. You are so kind." Ara pushed the remainder of the pottage and bread to the side to make room for eggs, applesauce, ham, and warm cider.

"You did not sup much last night," observed Mrs. Knecht looking at the contents of last night's meal.

Ara shook her head. "No, I was too nervous about meeting the king. I still am."

The servant saw before her a girl in a station similar to herself, and was curious. "Why is Lord Huber keen for you to meet the king? It is not often that a person of your class gets invited here."

"It is my cloth. Here, I will show you." Ara removed her red tunic from her bag. "I am able to spin my thread very finely and weave it into supple cloth." She passed the clothing to Mrs. Knecht to examine.

The woman took it from her and pulled it in all directions, rubbing it with her hands. "What thread is this made from? It isn't silk, but it's not anything I know."

"It's linen, thinly stranded."

"Oh, my. I've never seen such fine work made out of linen. No wonder the lord wanted the king to meet you. If you can teach others to make such a cloth, the kingdom would be enriched by their sales."

Ara blushed. She had taught Frieda to spin and weave, but she never thought of herself as a teacher to a group of spinners. *This could be a way for me to earn my living,* she thought. "Do you know when I will be permitted to see the king?" she asked.

Greta Knecht shook her head. "I cannot say."

CHAPTER 9

A servant opened the door to the king's chamber, and Lord Huber strode in and bowed. "Your Majesty, I have found a most remarkable young woman," he began, but was cut off by the king who was still in bed eating his breakfast.

"You are standing much too close." The king shooed him back with a lamb chop in his hand.

"Pardon, Sire, but this matter is such that I must speak with you closely and softly," spoke Huber. "You will understand in a moment."

The king waved him closer and wiped his mouth with a silk cloth. "Come then. Out with your news."

Huber stepped up to the bedside, and said in a low voice, "My Lord, I have brought a girl with me that can spin straw into gold."

"Bosh and hogwash, it cannot be!" exclaimed the king, spewing food across the bed linens. "I have never heard of such nonsense."

"It is true, Richard," insisted Huber. "Her father told me so. I did not believe it, either, until I saw a golden ring on her finger in the shape of wheat."

"I cannot believe such preposterousness!" The king climbed out of bed and towered over Huber. He was a young man, not yet thirty. His red hair matched his short temper. His icy eyes stared down at his subordinate. The deep blue of one and vivid green of the other never failed to disconcert Huber.

Huber insisted. "A miller could never afford a golden ring, yet she wears one. I believe that she is a strange alchemist."

King Richard considered the lord's statement. "Well, then, we shall have a test. If your miller's daughter can indeed spin straw into gold, I will give you one quarter of it. But if she fails, I shall have you whipped for bringing me such a story. Now, step back." He dismissed him off with the flick of his hand.

Lord Huber quickly took two steps back and bowed his way out of the chamber. When the door closed behind him, his heart was pounding. He mopped the sweat from his brow. *If the girl cannot spin, I will surely kill the miller,* he thought. He hurried to find a room he could fill with straw.

Ara was not allowed to leave her room. There was nothing for her to do but wring her hands and stay as calm as she could. She had changed into her red kirtle and threaded her hair with ribbon, just as she had done for the fair. *I do not even know how to greet the king,* she thought. She practiced curtseying, becoming more adept over time. She kept looking out the window and calling to Jana, but he was nowhere to be seen.

Evening was falling and Ara could see a gibbous moon in the sky. It was her favorite moon, big and slightly lopsided.

As she called for Jana again, he flew to the window. "Jana, oh Jana, come here," she entreated. He flew to her hands and she kissed his head. "Where were you today? I missed you, my friend." The black bird purred as best as a raven could. Ara sat on the bed with him in her lap.

Her back snapped up straight when she heard footsteps in the hallway outside her room. Jana fluttered up to the window, and flew away when the door swung open. Lord Huber stood in the doorway carrying a lamp. "Come with me," he ordered abruptly.

Obediently, Ara stood and went to his side. He took her arm. They walked briskly down two flights of narrow stairs and through a dimly lit hallway, the candles flickering in their stands. "How is my father? Are you taking me to him?"

"He is fairing well, Miss Miller, and is resting comfortably. You shall see him soon."

"When I meet the king, does he speak or do I address him first?" she asked.

"There has been a change in plans. You will meet the king tomorrow." He stopped at a dark, heavy, oak door and opened it. The cold from the room crept over her as she inhaled a musty odor. Huber bent down to place the lamp on the floor. As her eyes adjusted to the low light, she could see that the room was filled to the ceiling with straw. In a corner was a spinning wheel and stool. "In the meanwhile, you will spin this straw into gold by the morning," he ordered.

Ara stood aghast, her hand on her chest. "I cannot do that. It is impossible to do such a thing!" she cried.

"Your father claims it to be true. If you fail, the king will give me ten lashings." He stood nose to nose with her and growled. "And I will make sure you get fifteen." He thrust her into the room and slammed the door shut. She heard the key turn and footsteps fall away.

Ara pounded her fist on the door. "Let me out! I cannot spin straw. I cannot." she cried. Ara beat the door until her strength wore out. She fell to the stone floor and cried bitter tears. *How could Lord Huber believe such a silly man as my father? Mama, I need you now. Why did you die and leave me?*

There was then a sound, a soft brushing of the straw that caused her to look up. A strange, small, wizened man stood before her, his skin the color of olives and his black hair was streaked with gray. She would take him for a hunter with his dark woolen mantle over his tunic fitted with a belt. His hood fell to his shoulders and a leather cap sat upon his head. Frightened, she slid back against the door.

"I will not hurt you, young maiden." He took a step forward.

She crouched into herself, too afraid to speak. He spoke again. "Do not fear me. Tell me your trouble."

Ara found her voice. "Lord Huber told me I must spin this straw into gold, but I cannot. It is an impossible task." She was choking on her words.

The small man shook his head. "I can do it. Watch me." He grabbed a handful of straw and bent it around the distaff.

Then, sitting at the spinning wheel, he began treadling. Within moments, he spun shiny strands of golden thread. He brought it over for Ara to examine.

Ara took the gold thread in her hands. Her mouth dropped open. "Impossible," she breathed, "but you did it!"

The man nodded. "Will you spin for me?" she begged.

"How will you pay me?" he asked.

She slipped her golden ring off her finger. "This was my mother's and is very dear to me. Will you spin for this?"

He took the ring in his hands and examined its wheat design. Sliding it onto his finger, he assented. "Yes, I will spin for you, but you must help if it is to be done quickly."

Together they began working. As fast as she gathered the straw and tied it to the distaff with her hair ribbon, he spun it into golden thread. She wound it into coils and gathered more straw. They were finished in half the night. Ara looked around at the room. There was not one trace of straw left, only coiled gold in its place. She turned to thank the good man, but he was gone. She made a bed of gold and waited until morning.

She was standing when the door swung open and Lord Huber entered the room. "By Jove!" he exclaimed when he saw the skeins of gold thread. "You've done it! You've done it!" He grabbed Ara and twirled her around. "You are a miracle! Wait here." He slammed the door behind him, and Ara was alone once more. This time she wasn't afraid. Now she could meet the king and return home with her father.

Ara heard more footsteps and the clang of the key. The lord was followed closely behind by a tall man in silken clothing. She was struck by his appearance. Belstrumburg was a small town of only a few hundred people and the villagers' hair color ranged from blonde like her father's to dark brown like hers, but she had never seen red hair such as his before. The man bent down and grabbed several coils, letting them slip down his fingers. "Amazing! I did not think it possible, but it's true." He rubbed his hands together and laughed aloud. Only then did he look to Ara. "You must be the witch who did this magic."

"Oh, no, Sir, I am no witch. Please, I am just a miller's daughter." She was startled by his eyes. One was a leaf green and the other was as blue as the sky. She took a step back, frightened by such strangeness.

Lord Huber spoke up, "Ara, I would like to introduce you to your King Richard." Immediately, Ara curtsied low, not daring to look up. She was trembling from lack of sleep and being so close to the king.

The king raised her up. "Well, Miller's Daughter, you can spin magic. Come with me." King Richard escorted Ara up several flights of stairs and into a large chamber. It held the biggest bed Ara had ever seen. The bed and the walls were covered in deep blue silk. "You have spent the whole of the night spinning, so now you are to get some rest. I will have a servant bring you food." He quickly withdrew and returned to the room full of gold where Huber was waiting. The king's eyes gleamed.

"You are brilliant, my good man. You shall have your share in this." The king was gleeful. "Let us have more gold. Ara must spin again this evening."

Huber nodded in agreement. He suggested they find a larger room to fill with straw. The king guffawed and slapped him on the back. "Good thinking, my good man. Come, let's celebrate." With his arm slung across his treasurer's shoulder, the king walked mirthfully down the hallway.

Meanwhile, Ara was drawn a bath and napped fitfully tucked inside silken sheets. When she awoke hours later, new clothes of brocade were on the bench at the end of the bed. A servant came in and brushed her chestnut hair, weaving the ribbon back into Ara's plaits.

That evening, she dined with Lord Huber and King Richard in his solar. The king was in a jovial mood, laughing and drinking several cups of wine. He did not fail to notice how attractive Ara was once she was dressed in proper attire. She, however, was nervous and anxious to return home before it was discovered that she was not the spinner they thought she was. She bit her lips and picked at her food. Ara stole glances at the king. His ginger hair was uncommon in her village, and his eyes were stranger still. Beyond the odd coloring was a coldness in them that made her shiver.

When dinner was over, Lord Huber helped her push her chair back from the table. Standing, she asked, "Will the Knechts be taking my father and me back in the morning?"

"He is not well enough to travel, my dear," he replied. "Come with me. I will take you to him."

His grip was tight on her arm as they walked through the dark hallways. The rich wooden panels gave way to cold, stone walls as they descended into the bowels of the castle. She breathed in the mustiness of the dank stairway and twisted free. "Oh, no, Sir. Please, do not put me back in a room of straw!"

Lord Huber seized her by the waist and dragged her to a door. There, he flung it open and pushed her into the room. "One more night, Miller's Daughter. Spin one more night."

"No, no. I cannot. You do not understand!" she pleaded. "My father. I want to see my father."

Huber drew himself up and hissed into her face. "If you do not spin this straw to gold, you will return home with your father's corpse. Spin!" He whisked the door shut and turned the key. She faced the room. It was twice the size of last night's and twice as full. Her only hope was the strange little man from the night before.

"Sir, Sir," she called out to him. "Are you here? I need you." Tears welled in her eyes when she was met with silence. *Papa, what did you say to Lord Huber? Your exaggerations will get you killed.* She began to weep, but abruptly she stanched her tears with her fingers. She tied some straw to the distaff and sat at the spinning wheel. She treadled it, but the straw remained straw. Ara bent forward, defeated, her elbows on her knees.

From behind her the kind, little man spoke, "I am here to help you once more."

Ara wheeled around. "Thank you, thank you," Ara said, relief spreading across her face.

"But you must pay me something of value," said the man.

"I can give you this gown. It is made of silk and very expensive," she offered.

"It has no value to you. I want something precious of yours," he replied. "What else do you have?"

Ara's hands went to her throat, to her mother's necklace. You may have this." She reached behind her neck and unhooked the clasp. It was her most prized possession, but was not as valuable as her father's life. She placed the necklace in his hand and watched him examine it before he placed it under his cap.

"Let us get to work." Their routine was the same as the night before. She collected and tied the straw to the distaff while he whirred, the wheel spinning out threads of gold. It was a long night since there was twice the straw of the night before. Her fingers were chafed and she was weary from bending and coiling the whole night. Finally, she wound the last skein of gold. Shafts of light from the morning sun entered the window. Ara looked around. If the room was not a prison to her, she would have appreciated the beauty of the glistening gold stacked as high as she could reach. She did not try to count the rows.

Ara let out a long breath. "Thank you, sir. You have saved me once again." She extended her hand in thanks, but with a smile, he disappeared before her eyes.

Relief washed over her. The good man spared her father's life. The room was filled floor to ceiling with gold thread. She could not begin to calculate its worth. She sat on the stool and closed her eyes. It was not long before she heard footsteps once again. The door swung open and the king stepped inside. He laughed with delight when he saw the gold. His eyes swept each corner of the room. This was incredible. He heard stories of people turning metals into gold, but not straw—cheap, valueless straw.

Ara stood up. "I would like to travel home today with my father. I am very tired and want to be in my own bed."

"No, not yet. Come, let's get you comfortable. You are in no state for travel." The king put her arm in his and led her back to her bed chamber. "You will remain here for now. Get some rest."

"I was told..." Ara began, but the king shushed her.

"Forget what you were told," his voice was tinged with ice. "You will remain here." He stalked from the room.

Ara flung herself on the bed. She was supposed to be a guest, but now she was a prisoner. Would she ever get home? Jana flew into the room and landed on the bed. He hopped over to her. "Ara," he quawed. His deep throated chunking sounds comforted her. At least he was at her side. She slept for hours, but when she awoke, her bird was gone.

A chambermaid came in with new clothes for her. She helped Ara change and combed her hair into a bun at the nape of her neck, winding the ribbon around it. She placed a coif atop Ara's head. Ara hunched her shoulders and spoke only clipped sentences as the maid tried to forge a conversation. She felt defeated.

There was a knock at the door, and Lord Huber stepped inside the room. "I will take you to see your father." Briskly they walked up stairs and through several hallways. Finally, Huber escorted her into a small, windowless room. There, propped up in a narrow bed, was Peter. He was awake, but looked more jaundiced than before.

Ara knelt by his side. "There you are, my Ara." His cold hands clasped hers.

"How are you feeling, Papa?" She put her cheek against his.

He closed his eyes. "Tired, very tired. But I should be well soon. The doctor bled me, and that should help make me better."

"Get some rest, Papa. I will see you in the morning." Ara tucked the bedding tighter around him, and left.

Food was brought to her room, but she only managed a few sips of ale. Fear snaked through her at the thought of being ordered to spin once more. She longed for home. The king came alone and took her to a room that was even larger than the previous night's. Again, it was filled top to bottom with straw.

She drew back, but the king held her firmly. "Ara," he spoke kindly, "this is the last time I will ask you to spin. If you do this, you will make me the richest king of all." She hung her head in despair. He continued, "If the room is filled with gold when I return tomorrow, I will make you my wife." When she tried to wrench free, his breath got hot and his eyes became icicles. "If you do not comply, I shall take your head. I will not allow you to be alive and spin for anyone else." He dropped her arms and she covered her face with her hands. She heard the door lock behind her and footfalls fade away.

When at last she uncovered her eyes, the small, olive-skinned man stood before her. "We must get to work. The room is big. It will take all night to spin."

"Thank you, good man. I am forever in your debt." She reached for his hand and found it warm and comforting. "You have helped me these past two nights, but I don't even know your name."

"I am just a spinner. You may call me that."

She kissed his hand. "You are more than a spinner. You are a lifesaver."

The man acknowledged this with a touch to his hat. "However, you must again give me something you value." His gravely voice was low.

"I have nothing to give you. You have my mother's ring and necklace. They are all I own of value," Ara replied.

"Then give me your first-born son," said the man.

Ara stepped back, startled by the fee. How could one ask to give away a child? But it was an easy promise to make, to promise something she did not have, and, surely, if the task was not completed, it was something she would never have. "Agreed."

They set about in their established routine, but at a faster pace since there was twice the straw from the night before. Few words were spoken between them. Ara grabbed and tied and coiled all night long while the spinning wheel whirred nonstop. There was no time to think about her raw, stiffened hands and aching back. Birds were chirping and the sun was climbing up the trees when she heard the key turning in the lock. Jana, who spent the night unnoticed on the window ledge high up in the wall, flew silently away.

Ara shrunk back when the door flew open. The wheel was spinning and she was sure the little man was still at the treadle, but when she looked, all she saw was an empty stool. The king looked about, amazed. He laughed aloud. Skeins of gold filled the room. He was rich beyond compare. It would be impossible to spend all that gold in a lifetime, in two lifetimes.

He grabbed Ara, lifting her up and twirling her around. "I am overwhelmed, Miller's Daughter. I have never seen so much gold." He bent to his knee. "You are the most valuable person I know. I shall make you my queen," declared the king.

Ara had no words to speak. She knew the king would not let her go free as long as he thought she could spin straw into gold. If he discovered the truth about the little man, he would kill her for a lie that was her father's. She was trapped.

CHAPTER 10

"Why did you tell Ara you would marry her? She is just a peasant." Huber and King Richard were ambling through the gardens where no one could hear them. A mist was falling from silver clouds and a chill was circling around them. "If you marry another king's daughter, you will strike an alliance and strengthen your position."

"Yes, I know," agreed the king, strolling, his hands joined behind his back. "That had long been my intention. But Ara changes that. She is like the goose that lays the golden egg. She gives me unlimited wealth. I can buy all the allies I want, and I can spread the wealth so men will clamber to be my knights and vassals."

"Look how rich you are now. Surely you have all you need," said Huber, thinking about the gold the king promised to share with him.

"I had enough for this realm, but now I have riches enough to create a vast one. I want to conquer other kingdoms until I own all the land to the sea. I may never need more gold, but if word spreads of Ara's skill, another king would surely try to steal her to become richer and more powerful than I."

"You can imprison Ara," suggested Huber.

"If I imprison her, she might refuse to spin ever again. No, I must marry her to keep her compliant. Then no one will know her secret, except you and me."

"And her father," added Lord Huber.

"Yes, her father," repeated the king pensively.

The two men returned to the castle, each deep in thought. In just three days' time, Ara had changed their fortunes. They suppered together in the solar where they toasted each other's good fortune, and made plans for the gold to be melted into bars and struck into coins. Before parting, they clasped each other in a warm embrace. "I will return early tomorrow to my manor. I sent my servants ahead two days ago, and my wife will be wondering what has kept me," said Huber.

"I need you back within a week to manage the treasure," reminded the king. "The rooms of gold will be sealed until you return."

"I will be back within three days," promised Huber as he retired from the room. As soon as he was gone, the king called for the captain of the guards.

In the morning, Huber noticed the streaks of red beginning to show in the sky as he headed to the stables for his horse. He wondered if there would be a storm before he made it home. A groom helped him into his saddle, and he cantered off. He was found dead hours later by some travelers at the entrance to the forest path.

CHAPTER 11

The Cooper family was surprised when Ara wasn't waiting for them outside her home. It was Sunday and she never before failed to be standing by the doorway when they pulled up in the wagon.

"Perhaps," Frieda suggested, "she is taking a little more care because Klaus will be at mass." Frieda had gotten up earlier than usual to fuss with her hair and pinch her cheeks until they turned pink. "I'll hurry her up."

She jumped down from the back of the wagon and knocked on the door, but there was no answer. She walked inside calling her cousin's name, but was met with silence. She went up to Ara's room. The bed was neatly made. Nothing seemed out of order. Peter's room was empty as well. She rushed outside. "They are not here."

Her parents hurried from the wagon. Her father checked the barn before entering the house. "I don't think Ara was here this morning. Her bedroom window is still shuttered," said Frieda. She felt fear rising from the pit of her stomach.

Clare spied the writing tablet on the table. She read it aloud. " 'Papa and I have gone to see the king.' That's all it says. Mannus, go to the church and ask Lord Belstrum if he knows about Ara and Uncle Peter."

He took off in a run and paced impatiently for church to let out. When Lord Belstrum walked outside, Mannus stepped in front of him and bowed. The parishioners gathered near. In a rush, he told the lord of Ara's note.

A peasant and his wife stepped forward. "We saw them riding out of the village in the back of a wagon a few days ago. A nobleman on a big horse accompanied them. We waved, and the miller waved back."

Another peasant saw them, too. "I'm sure it was Peter and his daughter. I have seen her often enough at the mill."

"What did the man on the horse look like? asked Lord Belstrum.

"He was a portly man, clad in fine clothing. The horse was dressed with bells on its mane," replied the man.

Mr. Kauffman interrupted the group. "A nobleman bought some of Miss Miller's cloth from me on the first day of the feast. He said he was going to show it to the king, but maybe he took the two of them with him, too."

It must have been Lord Huber, thought Belstrum. His wife had shown him her linen. He must have taken Ara and her father with him."Today is the Sabbath. I will ride out to Lord Huber tomorrow to hear what he has to say." Belstrum moved away from the crowd, mounted his horse and spurred him on.

Lord Belstrum arrived at Huber's moated estate by early afternoon. He learned that Ara and her father had indeed traveled with Huber by wagon driven by two servants. They had returned to the estate two days ago, but the others remained at Lundgrin Castle. Belstrum bit the inside of his cheek. He nodded his thanks and set off once again.

He traveled for an hour before he came to the part of the road that skirted a forest. A peasant waved frantically for him to stop. "Sir, there is misfortune ahead. A nobleman lies dead," he called out.

Belstrum reared his horse to a halt. "Who is the man?" he demanded.

"I know not, but he is richly clothed. There are two men ahead who are with the body."

The lord spurred his horse and galloped on. He had traveled not ten minutes farther when he spied two men with the lord's horse. "What goes here?"

"An accident, Sir, or a murder. I cannot say," answered one of the men. "This fellow has been trampled or beaten to death."

Belstrum swept off his horse and examined the dead man. It was Lord Huber. His clothes were shredded and his arm was bent in an awkward angle. His face was badly bruised and his head was smashed in on one side. "Was there any sign of anyone with him?"

"We saw no one, Sir. We came across only him. There was no one else around."

Belstrum found the dead man's money pouch still attached to his belt. He untied it and withdrew several coins to give to each man. "Stay with the body. I will take the horse and ride to the castle to send someone for the lord."

He mounted his steed and trailed Huber's horse behind him. When he arrived at Lundgrin, he briskly handed off both horses and informed a guard of the dead man. He was escorted into the great hall and, soon after, into the throne room where the king sat in conversation with other men. Belstrum bowed low and asked to speak with him privately. The king dismissed the others with a flick of his wrist.

When they were alone, Belstrum told the king of Huber's death. "I don't think it was a robbery. His money bag and his horse were both with him. It may well be that he was thrown from his horse and trampled."

"Dead!" the king exclaimed. "Why he left here just this morning. He was anxious to get home." The king continued. "He was with me for several days. He mentioned that his horse was high spirited and difficult to handle." He called in his guards and instructed them to ensure Huber's body was brought back to the castle to be cleaned before transporting it back to his manor. "Don't return the horse. His wife will have it killed. I'll have it retrained."

"There is one more matter, Your Majesty. A man and his daughter from my village traveled here with Lord Huber. I don't know if they were returning with him when he was killed," worried Belstrum.

King Richard brightened. "Ah, Ara Miller and her father. Yes, indeed they are still here."

Lord Belstrum exhaled in relief. "Then they are safe. The whole of the village was worried."

King Richard walked down the steps from the throne and placed his arm around Belstrum's shoulder. "As lord of her village, you shall be the first to know and take back the good news to everyone there." He paused dramatically. "I am taking Ara as my wife."

"The miller's daughter?" The lord stepped back, incredulous. "Beg pardon, Sire. I am taken by surprise."

The king tilted his head back and laughed. "All of the kingdom will be surprised, but after meeting her, I could not want anyone else. Hurry back to Huber's family and send my sympathies. Let them know I will attend his funeral. Then give your village the news."

Belstrum bowed. "When I return to Huber's home, I will send word to the miller's kin that they are safe. May I see your betrothed and her father to give my hardy wishes to so fortunate a family?"

"Alas, her father has taken ill and she is with him now. Let her family know that the wedding will take place in a month's time. I will deliver your good wishes to them."

When Belstrum arrived to Huber's manor, he sent word ahead that the miller and his daughter were safe at the Lundgrin Castle. He remained for the burial before he returned to his village, going straight to the Cooper's home to give the news of the pending marriage. Clare was overwhelmed. "This is unbelievable news. Ara, to be queen!" She sat down hard on a bench. "I pray that my brother will get well quickly."

The lord then shared the news with the priest before returning to his manor. The priest immediately went to Mr. Kauffman. It did not take long after that for all of the village to learn of Ara's upcoming marriage to the king. Many didn't believe it, and thought it was careless gossip until it was formally announced in church the following Sunday.

CHAPTER 12

Ara felt like a bird in a cage suspended in the air. She wasn't free to move about the castle but was kept in her chambers until called upon, and was carefully watched when she visited her father. Seamstresses were sent to take her measurements in order to create a wardrobe fit for a queen. Her hair, which she usually kept under a coif, was now intricately braided. Sometimes flowers encircled her head, and other times jewels were woven into the plaits. She was given etiquette lessons and taught how to walk erect in her new shoes.

King Richard came to visit Ara each evening during the first week of their betrothal. He brought little gifts for her; a lace handkerchief, dried figs, a silk fan. She began to think that he might be a gentle man, after all.

One evening as they walked the dimly lit corridors of the castle, he could not rouse a smile to her lips. "You seem sad, my Ara," commented the king.

"My father is failing. He isn't eating and is sleeping most of the time. The doctor is bleeding him regularly, but it doesn't seem to be helping. He's very weak."

"I will talk to the physician. Maybe there is an elixir he can try." The king called for the doctor soon after he left Ara. "My wedding is in three weeks. Get this over now."

Peter Miller died the next day. Richard brought the news to Ara. She did not cry but sat quietly. "He is with my mother at last," she sighed. "It is all for the better for Papa."

The king informed Ara that a funeral mass and burial would take place the following morning. "This is what we do at Lundgrin," he lied to her. He wanted the service as far away from the wedding as possible. He had the priest consecrate a gravesite in the gardens. "You can visit your father whenever you walk among the flowers."

"You are kind, Sir. I am grateful for your thoughtfulness." They sat silent in thought, she remembering a past life with her parents, and the king wondering how much longer he needed to stay by her side to still be considered kind.

Ara awoke early for the funeral mass. She found Jana perched on the footboard of her bed. "You have been the one constant in my life, Jana. I don't know what I'd do without you."

The raven hopped over the covers to be closer to her. "Ara, love," he quawed.

"Shhhh, the Lady of the Chamber is coming to dress me. Go for now."

The candles threw shadows on the walls of the chapel. A crucifix hung behind the small altar, and above it was a mural depicting God in the heavens. Flowers had been placed on the altar and at the end of the pews. The walls rounded up to form the ceiling. Richard sat stiffly next to Ara. They were alone except for the priest. He had been ordered to hasten through the mass, but he kept a measured pace, much to the king's annoyance. A cold, pouring rain at the burial, however, spurred the priest to hurry the final prayers.

Richard led Ara to the solar where a breakfast had been placed. It was part of the king's apartment where he hosted his closest companions, and one day would be his family's private room. "I have a request," she began. She had been mentally practicing for a week. "I would like my aunt, uncle, and cousins at the wedding. They are all the family I have now."

"It is a small request. Of course they will be invited."

"There is more. I would like my cousins Frieda and Mannus to come live here." Richard was silent, so she continued. "I am very lonely here. Frieda could become my Lady of the Bedchamber. Then I could have a companion to help me fill my time. I think she will like the idea of living at Lundgrin. She can sleep in the bed in my antechamber, so she will take up no additional room.

"What duty do you want for Mannus?" asked the king.

"He is accomplished with the bow. He would make an excellent hunter," she replied.

The king considered this. He needed her to be happy enough here, if she were to do his bidding later on. "Let them be asked. I will have the request relayed to them. If they are agreeable, they can stay on after the wedding." He rose to let Ara know the conversation was ended.

When she was back in her chambers, she curled up on her bed losing herself in her thoughts. Ara was confident that her cousins would relish the opportunity to leave the small village behind. They will jump at the chance to live here.

As the wedding approached, many of the noblemen and women began arriving at the castle. They brought beds and furniture to fill the rooms they would occupy until after the wedding. Richard spent his days hunting with the men, and in the evenings they joined the ladies for games and dancing. Ara was shy and intimidated by the genteel manners of the women who fawned about her. She observed them closely in the first days and spoke little.

Finally, Lady Belstrum took Ara by the waist and led her to an alcove. She kept her voice low. "Ara, I can see that this is an overwhelming time for you. These women want to be in your good graces because, as queen, you will have access to the king's ear, or so their husbands have told them. It is wise to be wary of them. Keep them at a distance until you are sure you understand their motives. Do not show your insecurities, because some will take advantage." Lady Belstrum lifted Ara's chin. "You are a clever young woman. Show them your strengths."

Ara smiled gratefully, inhaling deeply and exhaling slowly through puffed cheeks. "Thank you, Lady Belstrum.

I've been in a whirl and it's been hard to catch my breath." She grasped her Lady's hand. "You and your husband have always been kind and gentle overlords of our village. I will put my trust in you, and you may put your faith in me." Together they returned to the others.

The courtiers broke into small groups to play games. Ara seated herself to play Table of the Four Seasons with Lady Belstrum and two Lords. She moved her green pieces tentatively at first, but then caught the eye of her Lady who nodded slightly. With a smile, she emboldened herself and played aggressively, sending the other's colored pieces back to their original positions. She laughed as she won the game. "I have played this with my cousins for many years. You do not have to let me win. I will be a worthy contender."

She rose from the table to join another group when the door banged open and the man filling the entryway roared, "Richaaarrrd!"

The king jumped up, bellowing, "Alfred, you have arrived at last!" He rushed into the man's outstretched arms and the two embraced, slapping each other on the back. He stood back to look at the large man. Alfred stood a full head taller and had a wider girth. What remained of his hair atop his head was faded copper, while his beard was heavily sprinkled with white. He quickly dispensed with his cloak and hat, handing it over to one of the servants who was setting up the supper tables.

"I want to meet your betrothed," he demanded. "As your closest relative, you should want my approval." He scanned the room, settling his eyes on Ara who met his glance with a steady gaze. "Ah, look at this beauty!" his voice boomed. "She is far too good looking for a scoundrel like you." She felt her cheeks warm.

A slight woman stepped forward into the room. "Richard, you are as handsome as ever," she smiled broadly and curtsied low.

"Clotilde, your charm has never wavered," the king smiled, raising her to her full height that reached no further than his shoulders. He entwined her arm with his and brought her over to Ara.

"Ara, I present Princess Clotilde," and he stretched out his arm to Alfred, "and this lug of a man," he laughed, "is my cousin Prince Alfred."

Ara bent her knee and bowed her head. "It is my pleasure to meet both of you." She looked questioningly at Richard. She had not heard of these family members and made a mental note to ask Lady Belstrum about them.

The new guests supped at the same table with Alfred at Ara's side. "You are cousins?" questioned Ara, leading him into conversation.

"Indeed, I am," the prince responded amicably, showing a row of uneven yellow teeth. "Our fathers were brothers. Richard's, of course, was the elder of the two, but I am older than your soon-to-be-husband by five years. His father died when he was merely twelve, and my father served as his regent until he reached the age of eighteen nearly twelve years ago, now."

"I beg your pardon, Sir, but I did not know anything of this."

"Now it is time for me to beg pardon," Alfred responded. "You are not of noble birth and not much more than a child. Sixteen, I understand?" Ara nodded. "Your parents most likely did not bother with the concerns of royalty when it had no impact on your daily life."

It was true. She never heard Peter speak of the king except to complain about taxes. "I will learn quickly. Where do you reside?"

"I have several estates, but my main home where my children live is in Northrum. It's about one hundred miles from here, so Clotilde and I do not visit often." Ara sipped her wine. She had nothing to add to the conversation, but Alfred was not finished. He leaned in and spoke just above a whisper. "Be wary of Richard's temperament. He can be jovial and kind, but he can also be cruel. I have seen it with my own eyes."

As have I, thought Ara.

Alfred sat back and patted his wide stomach. Bending back in his chair, he called out, "Cousin, let us have some music for dancing. My legs demand it."

Ara asked Lady Belstrum to walk with her back to her chamber. "Please come inside," she requested and secured the latch carefully behind her. They walked to the wall farthest from the door. "I had an interesting conversation with...one of the guests," she spoke into the Lady's ear. "He gave me some advice about the king." Ara paused. "I am wondering if you had any advice to offer me about the king, too."

The room remained silent, and Ara was afraid her confidant would remain silent. Lady Belstrum opened and closed her mouth before finally speaking. "Did you know that snakes can lay about docilely, but will attack swiftly when provoked? They may even attack when unprovoked. It is always wise to stay clear of snakes and the cousin of snakes." She reached out to stroke Ara's cheek. "My husband and I are returning to the village to ensure your family's safe travels here for the wedding. I will see you then. Sleep well, my child."

CHAPTER 13

The day dawned crisp and clear on the morning the Coopers set out for the wedding. The family bustled about greeting the many villagers who came by to give their best wishes and fond farewells to Mannus and Frieda, as well as ogle the shiny black coach with big, red wheels that Lord Belstrum sent for them. Two strawberry roan horses waited patiently at the head of the coach. Aunt Clare watched as trunks were loaded onto the back. Their friends felt bittersweet to see them leave. There was much handshaking and hugging before the Coopers settled themselves into the cushioned seats. "Give our best wishes to Ara," called Mrs. Becker as the coach jolted forward. "Let her know we will never forget her in this village."

They traveled in tandem with Lord and Lady Belstrum who waited for them alongside the road. The nobles' carriage led the way with the horses at a steady trot. Frieda and Mannus were as excited as bears breaking into a hive full of honey. Not only were they off to begin a new life at the Lundgrin Castle, but they were going to see Ara wed the king. While Aunt Clare and Uncle Jasper were delighted about the marriage, the death of Peter had subdued them. Aunt Clare, in particular, wanted to put her arms around Ara and hold her in her sorrow.

When they arrived at the castle, the Coopers huddled together in the corner of the great hall as they took in the vastness of the room. The room was filled with servants scurrying about putting up banners and setting flowers along the many tables in preparation of the wedding celebration. They saw a noblewoman approach, and if Ara didn't cry out, they would not have recognized her. They were astonished by the change in her appearance in such a short time as four weeks. She had left Belstrumburg in a loose linen smock and woolen kirtle and greeted them in a fitted silk gown. Her long flowing hair was captured and roped by pearls in the back of her head.

Ara alternately laughed and cried when she was once again in the arms of her family. Here is where she felt the comfort and security of love these last years. She embraced each member tightly, clasping her aunt the longest. The tears she didn't shed when her father died fell freely now. The Coopers reeled with feelings of grief for Ara's father, and incredulity that she was to become queen.

She escorted them up the stone stairways and through the corridors to her antechamber where they had privacy and could speak freely. The small room was richly appointed with wooden panels hung with tapestries and portraits. Cherubs and clouds floated on the ceiling. The men stood frozen to the floor looking at the richness of the woods and paintings, but

Aunt Clare and Freida went around the room touching the fabrics of the chairs and tapestries.

"I have never seen so many chairs in my life," exclaimed Aunt Clare, "and they are filled with soft stuffing! Oh, what a comfortable life you will lead."

Ara made no comment about her loneliness and settled them at a table filled with meats and cheeses and wine and squeezed her chair in between her aunt and uncle. The aromas of the foods sharpened their hunger after their long trip. "How did it come to be that you are marrying the king?" asked Aunt Clare, piling her plate with foods she had only dreamed of eating. "We were in awe when we first heard the news."

"It was Lord Huber who brought me here to show the king my linen cloth," replied Ara. She could never reveal the part her father played in it. "Richard and I met and he decided he wanted me as queen."

"Was it love that brought the two of you together?" asked Frieda, a romantic at heart.

"Well, yes, in a way," Ara replied, thinking of the king's love of gold. She kept her eyes on her plate and quickly turned the conversation elsewhere.

The family told her of the excitement of the entire town when they learned she was to become queen. "Everyone is happy about it, except Klaus Becker," remarked Mannus.

Ara wanted to know about everyone, especially Mr. Kaufmann. "When he learned about your betrothal, he actually began sobbing. He was so overcome with relief and joy at your good fortune, he needed to be carried from the church."

They supped and talked until the travelers' eyes began to droop. Ara escorted them to their chambers and bid them a good night. "I will look for you tomorrow."

Jana was waiting at her window. "It is very late for you to be here," Ara said. "Stay with me until morning." The bird perched on the foot of the bed until dawn cracked.

A knock on the door signaled servants carrying buckets of hot water. After her bath she waited for the arrival of her wedding attire. She had spent her sixteen years wearing a linen smock with a kirtle laced over it. Woolen stockings and square-toed shoes completed her outfit except in cooler weather when she pinned a partlet onto her shoulders and long sleeves to the short ones of the kirtle. Occasionally she would don a woolen gown for church. Since she has been at Lundgrin, however, her clothing had become more elaborate. Two ladies came to dress her, and Frieda, who would be the Lady of the Bedchamber from tonight on, was there to observe the long procedure.

Ara felt tugged and prodded like a barnyard goat being led to slaughter. The women pulled silk knitted stockings over her legs, and tied them with garters. A white smock was slipped over her head and she was then made to step into a petticoat to add fullness to the gold kirtle that went over her next. The women laced it on both sides of her bodice to keep its neckline of emeralds and pearls unbroken. New, flat, green leather shoes were buckled to her feet. A coif was placed over her plaited hair that had been worked around the back of her head. A heavily embroidered green silk gown lined in sable fur was slipped like a long coat over her shoulders, exposing the kirtle beneath. The long, wide sleeves were folded back to display the fur. Foresleeves made of the same material as the kirtle were tied to the gown. Last, the Ladies draped a simple, short, white silk veil atop her head. Ara was ready for the ceremony.

Frieda stood in awe of Ara. "You look like a true queen," she breathed.

People lining the streets of the town shouted and clapped as Ara's coach rode to the cathedral. Lord Belstrum sat across from her as she stared straight ahead. The citizens were thrilled that the king had chosen a commoner, one of them, for his wife, instead of a foreign bride selected to forge an alliance with another kingdom. They loved her without knowing her.

Noble men and women stood along the steps of the cathedral forming an aisle. Ara was escorted by Lord Belstrum to the massive door where the king waited with the bishop. The king took her by the elbow and both turned to the bishop. It took just minutes to perform the simple wedding ceremony. The bishop next removed Ara's veil and coif and placed a crown upon her head. When the king faced the crowd and presented his queen, the shouting voices hurrahed and the church bells rang.

The king and Ara made their way to an awaiting gilded carriage to make its slow climb among the throngs to the castle. He waved as they shouted his name and instructed Ara to do the same. "Show them how happy you are to be their queen," he instructed. Their carriage stopped at the castle door as other carriages arrived for the wedding banquet.

She was swept inside by Richard and they made their way to their seats at the head table. She scanned the crowd searching for her relatives, finally spying them at the table with Lord and Lady Belstrum. They raised their glasses to her, and finally, her eyes creased as she smiled.

The rest of the day was a blur. Ara lost count of the courses served at the wedding banquet; roasted boars, fish, pheasants stuffed with raisins, swans, mutton, beef, ducks, geese, and venison. Puddings, tarts, custards, patties, wafers, and marzipan cakes were piled on the tables. Musicians strolled through the hall with pipes and mandolins and recorders. Voices and music bounced off the walls creating a cacophony of sounds.

At last Richard turned to Ara. "It's time for you to remove yourself to the chamber." He stood and raised her from her seat. With a low curtsey, she dismissed herself. Frieda joined two ladies in waiting who escorted Ara to her new apartment where they silently undressed her.

When Ara was in her bedclothes, and the two ladies dismissed themselves, Frieda and Ara embraced. "It is hard to believe that you are queen!" exclaimed Frieda.

"It is hard for me, as well," replied Ara.

"It is all wonderful. Mannus and I thank you for the opportunity to work here. It should be more exciting than the village."

"I am sorry that you will have to treat me as a better and curtsy to me," apologized Ara, "but it is the only way to keep you near me." She squeezed her cousin's hand.

"Do not worry about that. When others are around, I will treat you as a proper queen, but," Frieda winked, "when we are alone, you will merely be my same cousin."

"That is what I want. I do not want you or Mannus to forget who I am, and I want to have your mother and father visit us as often as they can."

Frieda nodded. "Are you ready for tonight? Are you instructed?"

Ara stiffened. She had been told the basics of the wedding night, and it seemed a terrifying task. "Yes, I am ready. You must leave me now. Richard will be here soon. I will ring for you in the morning. Stay with your family tonight and come to my apartment tomorrow for breakfast. I want us all together before your parents leave."

"We rode in tandem with Lord Belstrum. What if he wants my parents to depart early?" worried Frieda.

Ara grinned. "I am the queen. He must wait for me now." Frieda clapped her hands and laughed.

Richard left the chamber after Ara fell asleep. She was awakened by Jana's croaking at the window. She slipped out of bed and opened the shutters. "Hello, my friend. How did you find my new bedroom?" She shook her head. "You are an amazement to me." She crawled back in bed with the bird by her side and looked around. The walls in her large room were painted red with an overlay of a darker red diamond pattern. The bedcovers wore a matching design. Green silk drapes fell on either side of the ornately carved poster bed. On the ceiling Greek goddesses reclined on their sides. Bouquets of flowers were painted in the corners.

Ara's apartment included a bathroom with a black and white tiled floor. A bathtub stood ready to be filled with buckets of hot water, and she had a selection of oils to perfume the water. There was a carved wooden toilet with a chamberpot fitted below the seat.

Her antechamber was larger than her bedroom. Tables, settees, and cushioned chairs were arranged in small groupings so that Ara could entertain large groups or a few guests. Ceiling to floor windows filled one wall, and paintings and bucolic murals covered the others. A bed was placed in a corner where Frieda would sleep each night. As Lady of the Bedchamber, she would dress and undress Ara each day and be her closest confidant.

"Good morning," Ara greeted her cousin.

Frieda jumped up as the bedroom door opened and hurried to Ara. "Did all go well last night?"

"The deed is done," Ara sighed. "It was painful but quick." She slipped her arm through her cousin's. "I am captured for good."

"To be captured by a king is better than captured by a baker."

"Perhaps," replied the new queen. "Let me dress quickly so that we may eat with your family."

The Cooper family had some surprises from home to present to Ara. First was her bedroom chest filled with her clothes and tokens she had saved over the years. The next was the bag of flax seeds she had saved from this year's crop, and last was her spinning wheel. Ara closed her eyes to keep tears from spilling. "You brought my most precious treasures," she exclaimed.

"Sig will take over your cottage now that he is the new miller," said Uncle Jasper. "He will keep the loom for you until you send for it, but wonders if his wife can use it until then."

"Please let him know he may keep it as well as anything else in the home. He was good to my father, especially these last years."

"Then it is time for us to part. Lord Belstrum will be waiting for us." Aunt Clare's calmness was betrayed by the wringing of her hands.

"Wait just a moment," Ara requested. She hurried over to her chest and opened it. Digging to the bottom, she retrieved her bag of coins. "Take this," she said, enclosing it in her aunt's hands. "This is little to say thank you, but it is my earnings from my cloth." Their embrace was long.

The family walked together to the carriage that would take them home. Lord and Lady Belstrum stood apart near their carriage. Ara walked over to them as Mannus and Frieda said their private farewells to their parents. "Thank you for bringing my family to me. I am in your debt."

The lord bowed and his wife curtsied, promising Ara's aunt and uncle's safe return. "Please watch over them for me," she asked, "and whenever you come again, bring them with you if they are able to travel."

"You have my word on it," he assured her.

Returning to her family, Ara, Mannus, and Frieda watched as her aunt and uncle settled into the carriage. "Have a safe journey home," said Ara, "and please visit often."

Ara and her cousins stepped back and waved as the carriages clattered off. "Well then," Ara said, "we three begin a new chapter in our lives."

Frieda went off with Mannus to help him settle into his new rooms near the stables. Ara walked through the gardens alone to contemplate her new life. She would never have to provide for herself again, but being queen had cost her freedom of movement. In truth, her cousins would have an easier life and have the ability to come and go at will. She did not have a choice of husband. Richard had demanded that she wed him to keep her from spinning gold for anyone but him. Ara was fearful of him. Behind his carefully posed exterior dwelt a cruelty he could use swiftly. He already had been prepared to kill her. What would he do to her if he found out she couldn't spin straw into gold? She bent down and picked a rose. *My life is like this flower. It looks beautiful, but there is danger in the thorns.* She looked at her hands. One of her fingers was bleeding.

CHAPTER 14

The foundry hired more workers to mold the gold into bars and create new coins with the king's likeness stamped upon them. Once cooled, they were stacked in the treasury, a highly guarded building on the castle grounds. The king visited frequently to gleefully watch the stacks grow. Before Ara arrived, the gold reserve filled half of one room. Now three were filled to capacity, stacked row upon row from one wall to another. He shared his riches with his nobles, not because he was generous, but because he needed them to supply more knights, foot soldiers, pikemen, archers and crossbowmen along with weapons, horses, and armor.

King Richard's plan was to conquer all the kingdoms to the north and west until he reached the great seas. He formed alliances with kingdoms to the east and south, trading gold for loyalty and mercenaries. *Fools*, he thought. *I will vanquish them next and create a great empire.*

When the king was home, the nobility sought Ara out. She learned to play board games and dance. She drew and painted and embroidered. The activities were new to her and she found most of them stressful and boring. What she didn't do was spin and weave, as they were deemed crude tasks and below her station. She looked forward to the early morning when Jana would greet her. He couldn't spend more than a few minutes with her now that there were many people surrounding her.

Frieda brought her breakfast in bed each morning. Ara would turn the tray sideways while her cousin climbed upon the high bed to share her meal and talk about their plans for the day. Sometimes Frieda helped Ara with her sketches that she would be working on later. Frieda never knew she had an aptness for drawing because she never had paper before, but she had a keen eye and steady hand.

Ara was interested in how Frieda was getting on with the servants in the castle. "Friendships are coming slowly," Frieda said. "They know we are cousins and they are wary of me, but my stay here is still new. They are polite but cautious. I will win some of them over in time."

"I do not want this to be a difficult situation for you. You are here as a favor to me," said Ara.

"The king having a queen is new to everyone around here. You will not feel new to the servants in a year's time. Neither will I. Meanwhile I am actually enjoying the wariness. It is giving me an opportunity to see who will like me for myself. Also, this position is much more favorable than being in Belstrumburg under the eye of my parents. Come now, call the maid for a bath. Then I'll get you dressed."

Frieda was ready with the many layers of Ara's clothing when she left the bathroom. She dressed Ara from stockings to smock to kirtle to gown. It was much simpler attire than the wedding, but the fabric was still silken and luxurious.

"Draw with me at the lesson today," suggested Ara as she placed a coif and folded veil over her head. "You are clever with a pencil, so I think this will be an interesting occupation for you."

"No, I could not," protested Frieda. "I would feel foolish with the noblewomen there."

"You are higher in rank than a mere servant. Before you arrived, Ladies of the Court were dressing me. You should think of yourself as one of them. They won't know what to make of you, but we will teach them." Ara grinned. "If I am a miller's daughter who became queen, you can be a cooper's daughter who becomes a lady." She pulled Freida to her wardrobe and chose a gown for her. "Put this on. You only need to look the part to be halfway accepted. Your personality and your talent will supply the rest."

Freida impressed the ladies with her innate talent and quick wit, and Ara was happy to have her by her side. Later, when they were back in the antechamber eating a midday meal, Freida was quiet. "Did you not like today's activity?" asked Ara. She took a sip of wine and set down the goblet. "It seemed that you did."

"Oh, I did, very much," Freida answered. "I think, though, I should like to live a less complicated life, at least for now. I know who I am, and I am like this dress." She gestured to the simple gown she had changed back into after class. "This is how I'm comfortable."

"Would you like to return to Belstrumburg?" worried Ara.

"Goodness, no!" Frieda's response was quick. "Here the food is tastier, my bed is softer, and my clothes are nicer. There are more interesting men here, too." She held up a piece of venison with her knife. "It's against the law for we common folk to hunt in the forest, so I had never eaten this meat before coming here. I'm not going to give this up." She took a bite and chewed slowly. "Besides, you are my dearest companion and you are here, not in Belstrumburg."

"Very well." Ara reached over and stroked her cousin's face. "It's Wednesday. Mannus will be here to sup with us tonight. We shall learn how he is faring."

Mannus joined them once a week for what was always a convivial supper. He was one of the king's hunters, but also worked in the stables as a groom. His tall, slim stature and blonde hair attracted the attention of several of the young female servants. He kept Ara and Frieda laughing with stories about his work and his flirtations.

One of their favorite stories he told involved a bird. "Do you know the nightjar?" he asked.

"Yes, of course," replied Ara. "It comes out at dusk. It starts out with a 'chonk-chonk-chonk' sound and then its song. Well I can't properly call it a song; it's a long 'chaweaaa' with no break in between."

"That's a good imitation, Ara," approved Frieda. "Its call is more like a small frog's or even an insect's."

"That's it," said Mannus. "Mama said when we heard it, we had to go inside soon because darkness would fall soon after. Well, I was out near the stables one day and I heard it. I commented on the call of the nightjar, and one of the stable-boys corrected me. 'Oh, no, sir,' he said, 'that is the sound of the goatsucker.' 'Goatsucker,' says I. 'I've never heard of such a thing.' Another fellow agreed with the first. 'Aye, that bird will suckle at the teat of a goat.'"

The young women laughed until tears fell from their eyes. "I've never heard of such a thing, either," said Ara.

"Well, that is what our common, boring nightjar is called around here. Perhaps we should tie up a nanny goat and watch her all night."

CHAPTER 15

King Richard's visits to Ara slowed after the first month. He was away most of the time either visiting his other castles or at the nobles' manor houses discussing war plans. When he was gone, the court departed, as well. Several of them traveled with the king, while others returned to their manors. As a commoner, Ara held no use for them and they didn't find her amusing. The dancing and game playing came to a halt, and so Frieda and Ara began private lessons for drawing and painting.

One evening, Ara sighed and put down her embroidery needle. "I miss my spinning. It reminded me of my mother and gave me great comfort."

"Then let us spin," said Frieda. "Surely there must be a spare spinning wheel around here that I can use, and I can bring yours from where I stored it."

Ara's eyes lit up. "Let's go find a chamber where we can spin undisturbed. There are plenty of vacant ones in this huge place."

Laughing, the two young women went searching the castle for an unused room. They found one that suited their needs on the floor below. It was simply appointed with heavy velvet drapes and a few settees and chairs lined up against the walls. The parquet floor was bare of rugs .

Frieda arranged to have bags of hackled flax delivered, and in three days' time, the two of them were sitting at their wheels spinning. "This is delightful," said Ara contentedly. "This is what I needed to feel at home."

The cousins developed a routine, painting and drawing lessons in the morning, walking in the gardens in the afternoon after the sun chased away the winter chill, and spinning in the evening. Ara began French and geography lessons while Frieda mingled with servants, making friends along the way.

Richard was not missed. In truth, Ara did not know him well at all. She did not consider him a husband in the way her mother had thought of her father. He was detached from her when he was back at the castle, and the memory of his threat to kill her had not faded. He did not spend every night with her, and she suspected, but did not care, that he had mistresses elsewhere.

One day, as the two were walking arm in arm after visiting Peter's grave, Frieda looked sideways at her cousin. "I have an idea." The air was warming and had the scent of a recent rain. The trees were leafing out and buds were beginning to show. "You helped me become a better spinner. You were patient and guided my hand until I could spin a thread as thin and strong as yours. You have a knack for teaching. Why don't you hold a spinning class for the servants? It can be held in the evenings."

Ara stood still, her face brightening. "That's a splendid idea! If I can improve their skill, they might even be able to sell some of their fabric in shops, just as I did with Mr. Kaufmann."

Frieda spread the word about the class, and five woman showed up the following week. Ara had arranged for a dozen spinning wheels to be placed in the room but was undeterred by the low number of students. She understood many would be nervous about such close contact with the queen.

The class was successful. The women were able spinners, but under Ara's teaching, their threads became smoother and finer. The next week nine young women showed up, and the following week all the spinning wheels were being used. Ara was without pretense. She wore only her smock and kirtle and looked like every other woman in the class. Within the room, it was easy for the women to forget Ara's position. Her voice was moderate and her hand over theirs while she showed how to pull a thin thread felt warm and friendly.

"Why not expand the class?" Frieda asked while she was undressing Ara for bed one night. "We have nothing taxing to do with our evenings. We could hold classes two or three times a week, and we could invite the peasants' and villagers' wives. They all need to spin to make their families' clothes."

"Let's do it. I have another idea, too." Ara was excited. "You brought me my flax seeds. We'll plant them and teach them to make the fabric from seed to weaving. My seeds are much better than ordinary ones. If we keep growing and harvesting the seeds, they can be shared with others who can end up with better cloth."

That was how the town gained a reputation for the high quality of its linen. It took several years. In the beginning the amount of fine linen produced was small because most of the flax was left to ripen the seeds. The peasants shared the seeds with their each other to maintain the high quality flax. Ara and Frieda would go into the fields dressed in their simple clothes from Belstrumburg to help plant and weed whenever Richard was away. They harvested the flax and bundled and stooked them with the peasants. When it was time to ripple the seeds and ret the stalks, Ara and Frieda worked alongside them. It became a happy little party.

Ara liked the last parts of flax processing the best, because they could work in small groups laughing and talking while they used the breaks and scutching boards to get to the fiber. They sat while they brushed the flax using finer and finer hackle boards. Ara showed them how she combed the shortest fibers to get even more product. "For the finest linen, use only the longest fibers," Ara advised. "Don't mix them with short fibers. You can sell the fabric from the long fibers at a higher price. Save the other fibers for cloth used to make work shirts and family smocks."

To the spinners, she said, "Now the threads need to be scoured. You need to boil the skeins with water mixed with soda ash to rid them of their waxiness and impurities. You'll do this repeatedly until the water runs clear. Then you will boil them again for an hour to make them as white as possible and for the thread to take a dye." Following Ara's instructions, the women were amazed at how their threads looked. Linen could be hard to dye, but their skein colors were deeper and brighter than they had ever seen.

Looms were set up in another castle room where women taught others how to weave. After becoming proficient, some of them purchased looms of their own and set them in their homes. The older women, though, liked the companionship of other weavers and would weave comfortably side by side.

The town set up a linen guild and sold their cloth throughout the kingdom. Ara and Frieda were pleased with its success. "You have enriched this town," remarked Frieda. She was feeding Jana some pieces of trout Mannus had caught and cooked up for them. She had found the bird in Ara's bedroom one day and Ara swore her to secrecy. It had been too difficult to hide the bird since Frieda slept one room away.

"My dear cousin, the linen guild is the result of your idea of teaching how to spin in the first place. We have an admirable number of spinners now. Weavers, too."

Frieda began to speak and then stopped. She took a breath and began again. "I have something to tell you." Ara looked at her expectantly. "I have met someone."

Ara raised her eyebrows. " Frieda Cooper, are you in love?" Frieda nodded. "I am."

Ara pulled her to the settee. "Tell me about him."

"His name is Hans. He is a merchant who buys from the guild. Well, his father owns the shop, but Hans will inherit it. I met him when I went to town with a couple of our weavers. We were attracted to one another right away." Frieda blushed.

"Look at you. Your face is all red!" Ara exclaimed. Her eyes began to fill with happy tears. "How long ago did you meet?"

"Six months ago."

"Six months, and I'm just finding out now?" Ara's voice was louder than she intended. Jana croaked loudly and rustled his feathers.

Frieda became alarmed and moved away from Ara. "I'm sorry, Cousin. I just wanted to be sure. I...I didn't want to look foolish in front of you."

Ara grabbed her cousin's hands and put them to her lips. "Forgive me, Frieda. I was just taken by surprise. I am delighted for you, truly. Will you bring him to our Wednesday supper? Then Mannus will be here. Your brother can bring his betrothed, too, and we will have a little party."

The Wednesday suppers now included Hans and Mannus' fiancée, Marie, the daughter of one of the horse trainers. At first she was shy and intimidated being in the company of the queen, but Ara's friendly manner soon put her at ease. Her keen sense of observation and quick wit had everyone in the group laughing. These spirited dinners were the highlight of Ara's week.

CHAPTER 16

Since Ara's wedding six years ago, Aunt Clare and Uncle Jasper had been coming to Lundgrin twice a year to celebrate Easter and Christmas with their children and Ara. Once King Richard joined them, but he was away this winter holiday season invading other kingdoms.

It was late evening when a servant let Ara know they had arrived, and she and Frieda hurried out to meet the carriage graciously lent by Lord Belstrum. It was a happy reunion, just as it was each time. Ara set aside the same boudoir for them every year. There were always apples, cheese, honey, and wine waiting for them.

"I will go fetch Mannus. Frieda will stay here with you while you settle yourself," Ara instructed. "She'll bring you to my apartment when you are ready."

An hour later Mannus was anxiously sitting on the settee with his fiancée when his parents entered the antechamber. He quickly strode over to them, embracing his mother and shaking his father's hand. "You look well, both of you." He was grinning broadly.

"My son, you look handsome, indeed," said Uncle Jasper looking up and down at him.

Mannus was dressed in a smart gray jacket pleated at the bottom with black woolen breeches and stockings. He bowed. "Thank you, Father." He took his father by the elbow and reached back for his mother's arm, walking them over to the slight woman who was now standing nervously alone. "I would like you to meet my fiancée, Marie. Marie, my parents."

"How very lovely to meet you, Marie," smiled Aunt Clare, warmly. "We are looking forward to having you join our family."

"Thank you, indeed. I look forward to joining it." Marie looked over at Mannus who nodded approvingly.

A knock at the door brought forth Frieda with Hans. Introductions were made and wine was drunk. Soon the group was talking animatedly. A chiming clock let them know they were but fifteen minutes away to Christmas morning. "Let us go to mass in the chapel," said Ara. "When it is over, we'll come back here and sup. The month long fasting of Advent has made me hungry for rich food." Taking her aunt and uncle's arms, she led the small procession to the chapel.

Several people standing in the entrance of the chapel curtsied and bowed to Ara as she and her family entered and settled themselves into the front chairs. The others filled in the benches behind them. The chapel altar was decorated with fir boughs and apples. At the end of the mass, Mannus and Marie stepped before the priest who performed a wedding ceremony.

His parents gasped, delighted with the surprise. Before they could comment, Frieda and Hans stepped up and wed, as well. Aunt Clara began to cry and Uncle Jasper tried his best to hold back his tears.

The people sitting in the rows behind them came forward as Hans and Marie revealed them as their families. The aunt and uncle were overwhelmed. There were handshakes and hugs all around. All of them trooped back to Ara's antechamber for a lively celebration. Families were reintroduced since the shock of the marriages left Aunt Clare and Uncle Jasper's minds blank. Toasts were made and a small feast was eaten. Musicians entered and people danced. The sun was lighting the sky when the party ended. Carriages were called for the families, but Ara had arranged sleeping quarters for the newlyweds. They didn't gather at Ara's apartment for a Christmas meal until late afternoon.

"What a wonderful surprise for your mother and me," said Uncle Jasper as he toasted the newlyweds once again. "We hoped you would find helpmeets to make you happy, and both of you succeeded. Here's to a healthy life and healthy grandchildren." All the members of the family raised their glasses and drank.

When all the toasts were finished, but before the meal began, Ara rose. "I have an announcement to make." After a small hesitation, she declared, "I am with child." Frieda fairly screamed with delight, jumping from her chair to embrace Ara. Aunt Clare was right behind waiting for her turn.

"How long have you known?" asked her aunt.

"I suspected for a while. I am about four months along."
Ara laughed when everyone was settled again. "I was quiet
about it because I remembered my mother losing a child." She
was silent for a moment.

"You would think I would have noticed, dressing you
every day," blurted Frieda.

"I have the slightest bit of rounding right now, but just
wait. You will see soon enough."

"Does King Richard know?" asked Mannus.

"I am sending a letter to him tomorrow. I wanted my
family to know first." Ara looked around the table. These
were the people she loved, the ones who would love her child.
Gnawing in the recess of her mind, though, was her promise
to the Spinner. She must give her firstborn son to him. She
prayed for a girl.

CHAPTER 17

Whenever King Richard returned, he brought many noblemen with him, and others appeared when news of his arrival spread. As the number of occupants of the castle swelled, a myriad of workers were needed; maids, cooks, servers, grooms, hunters, and guards. Inversely, the numbers diminished while he was away. Ensuring income for the women dismissed during the king's absence had been the central reason for Ara to teach spinning techniques.

Christmas had passed, her aunt and uncle were back home, and Lundgrin was quiet except for the bustle of women who came to spin and weave. The women were now accomplished at their tasks, but they continued to meet for the companionship of others. It was a happy group of women who gathered several times a week. They came from the castle staff and from town.

They loved their young queen. She was one of them and good and kind, as was her constant companion, Frieda. Ara was sitting on a stool listening to a woman tell a funny story about her goat escaping when she felt the first flutterings of the baby. She sat up, not sure what she felt. Half an hour later, she felt it again. She stood and excused herself.

Back in her chamber she lay on her bed, her hands over her abdomen awaiting the flutters. She was exhilarated and terrified. What if this child is a boy? Ara tried erasing the thought from her mind, but it was useless.

Frieda slipped into the chamber a couple of hours later and found Ara still on the bed. "Are you not feeling well?" she asked. She sat on the bed next to her cousin.

"I can feel the baby move," Ara said in a voice so low, it was difficult to hear.

"Can I feel it?" Frieda put her hand on her cousin's abdomen but detected nothing.

"I can only feel it on the inside." Ara's sudden burst of tears alarmed Frieda.

She took her cousin in her arms. "Shall I call the doctor for you?"

"No," Ara sobbed. "I'm just afraid of having a baby." She could never divulge her terrifying secret. She cried until her head pounded. Frieda wet cloths and put them on Ara's forehead. Finally her tears subsided. "Thank you, my sweet cousin. I don't know what I would do without you." Ara climbed down from the bed and began undressing. "You need to go home to your husband. You've only been married a month."

"You and I agreed I would stay here three nights a week for now. Frieda slapped Ara's hand lightly and finished the task, handing her a clean nightgown. "Tonight I am here with you. Don't worry about me. I'll stay with you until you fall asleep." Exhausted from her fear, Ara began breathing the steady breath of sleep soon after she closed her eyes. Frieda watched her worriedly and then tiptoed off to her bed.

She lived in town with her husband above the shop. Hans would drive her up to the castle in the early morning, and Ara arranged to have her driven home on the nights she wasn't sleeping in the antechamber. Frieda relished the ride up, sitting beside her husband as the horses clomped up the road in the dark. They would sit cozily next to each other watching the shadows change shapes, wrapped in their winter cloaks with blankets around them and warmed stones at their feet.

Frieda would go directly to the kitchen to drink warm cider with the staff. Most of the women were part of the spinning group and greeted her affectionately. They would toast bread and sit and chat until it was time for her to go to Ara. She'd carry away a cup of cider and buttered toast for her cousin each time she left.

There was great excitement in the castle as word of Ara's pregnancy spread. It would be so for any queen, but the love the people had for her was palpable. Most employed there had worked under Richard's mother, the former queen. She had been haughty and removed from the staff. Ara knew most of them by name and smiled and touched their hands. They were pleased to serve her.

Frieda opened the window each morning to let Jana in. The bird would fly directly to Ara and call out her name. "Love Ara" he would say which never failed to bring a smile to her face. After breakfast and dressing her, Frieda took her out for long walks to distract her. They always stopped at Peter's grave first. Ara came to think of it as her mother's grave, too. She prayed and talked silently to both of them, but, in truth, mostly to her mother. *Help me, Momma. Make this child a girl.* Then they would continue on with Jana landing nearby, flitting from garden to garden until they reached the woods.

Ara liked walking in the woods. She felt cloaked by the trees. In the forest, she was Ara, the miller's daughter. The farther they walked into the woods, the freer she felt. Without fail, Frieda would be the one to suggest they return to the castle. Ara would not come out on her own.

After her fearful reaction to the first flutterings of life, Ara pushed her negative thoughts away. She added harp and history lessons to her classes to occupy herself. She was determined to keep her mind away from the sex of her baby. There was as much of a chance of being a girl as a boy, and she refused to dwell in the future. It would arrive soon enough.

The gardens were masses of color when Ara was about to enter her last month of pregnancy. She liked to roam through them and watch spiders crawl about the flowers. She would observe them for an hour or more while they swung from petal to leaf and spun a web strong enough to withstand a storm. *I am one of you. I am a spinner and weaver, too, my friends.* Frieda worried about her cousin walking too far. She had benches placed in the gardens so Ara could sit with her face to the sun. Ara grew quiet. She would close her eyes and imagine a simple life back in the village with Klaus Becker as her husband. She would work next to him in the bakery and spin and weave in the evenings. She imagined several children, none of whom would be taken away by a little man.

"My mother should be arriving tomorrow to await the birth of your child with you," remarked Frieda. She looked at Ara and frowned. Her gown hid much of the swell of her abdomen, but Frieda dressed her each morning and saw its size. Labor should begin within the month. Giving birth was sometimes deadly. She worried for her cousin.

Today was Ara's last day outside before she began the lying-in period. Ara kept her eyes closed. "I am glad she will be here soon. I want the two of you near me. How lucky you are not to be cut off from the outside as I am."

Frieda patted her arm. "I will stay with you for the whole month you're lying-in."

Ara sat up. "No." Her answer was firm. "Hans has been very good about not having his wife with him by his side these last months, but that is where you belong. Your mother will lie in with me and you will come and go. If you are not here when I begin labor, I will send for you quickly." Ara searched her cousin's eyes. "Richard has been away since before Christmas.

He has not felt the kick of this child. I am told he will travel halfway back here. If the baby is a girl, he will return to his army. Only if the baby is a boy will he come home. I would like to have a husband who is interested in me. You have that in Hans. Make him more important than me."

Frieda nodded. She had a husband who loved her. She liked the coziness of her home and the warmth of Hans in bed next to her. His light snoring was a comfort to her. It said, *I am here. You are safe with me.* Ara lived in a huge castle with an apartment twice the size of hers above the shop. Servants prepared Ara's food and cleaned for her. Everyone but the king curtsied to her, but she could not move freely about. The lying-in would confine her even more. She would never want to trade places with Ara.

"It's time to get ready for the service in the chapel," sighed Ara. "The priest will ask God for His blessing to keep me safe during childbirth." She said goodbye to Jana who was hopping about. "I will not be able to leave my apartment until ten days after the birth of my baby. Make sure you visit me every day." The bird jumped to her shoulder and pecked her on the cheek. She petted his head and he spread his wings and flew off towards the woodland.

They returned to Ara's apartment to change into the last gown she would wear until after the baby was born. According to the custom for a queen's pregnancy, tapestries now covered the windows in all the rooms except one in her bedchamber to ensure too much light didn't damage Ara's eyes. "This lack of light won't do my embroidery work any good," she commented.

Frieda was careful dressing Ara, making sure the laces on her kirtle were tied loosely before she slipped the gown over her shoulders. Together they made their way to the chapel. Lord Richtmann, King Richard's chancellor, was there as were other lords and ladies who arrived to watch the blessing ceremony. Ara had not seen many courtiers in recent months so she was surprised by their appearance. They each held a candle during the ceremony. She could smell the burning wax mingled with the woody scent of incense. When she knelt at the altar, she felt her first chill of fear about childbirth. The ceremony reminded her that labor was painful and dangerous to both mother and child.

After the service was over, Ara was overwhelmed to see the women who spun with her lining the corridor to her apartment. As she walked past them, each one bowed and said, "Bless you, my queen."

When she reached her rooms, Ara turned to them. "Thank you. You have all been a blessing to me." She then did the unexpected. She curtsied back to all of them and entered her room.

Ara leaned against the door of her antechamber and looked around. Crucifixes, rosaries, and statues of saints were scattered on tables for spiritual support. Frieda was waiting for her at the door of the bedchamber. "Are you ready?" she asked.

Ara took a deep breath and nodded. "I must do this, so I am." Together they went into the chamber. A crucifix hung on the wall across from the bed and a Madonna with Child statue stood on a bedside table. Frieda undressed her and slipped a nightgown over her head. Ara got into bed where she was supposed to remain until labor began. "In the village I have seen many women walking about several days before giving birth. I do not see why I have to stay in bed for weeks. I will go mad."

"None of those other women were giving birth to the king's child," reminded Frieda. She removed the bolster from behind Ara and put fluffed feather pillows in its place. "You can embroider on the baby's gowns and bonnets to keep you occupied. You can knit, too. My mother will keep you company, as will Marie and I. Some of the ladies will visit you, too. You can draw with them and they'll play music for you. The time will pass."

"I will have to tell your mother about Jana. There is no way to hide him, and I don't want to send him off for a month."

"I will be here when you tell her. I want to see her face. Wait until she finds out he has been with you all your life!" Frieda laughed. "Good night now. I will see you in the morrow." She kissed Ara and dismissed herself from the room. One of the Ladies of the Court would stay with Ara tonight.

Lord and Lady Belstrum drove Aunt Clare to the castle the next evening. Frieda immediately brought her to Ara. "Let me look at you," said the aunt. Dutifully, Ara pushed back the bedding, and pressed her nightgown to her belly. "Oh, my," beamed Aunt Clare. "It won't be long now."

Ara laughed and gave her aunt a hug. "Thank goodness you are here. Are you sure Uncle Jasper doesn't mind?"

"He'll be fine. We have an apprentice living with us now, and the two of them are companionable."

"We will have supper together, and then I will head home after I settle my mother into the antechamber for her stay," said Frieda. "Tomorrow a midwife is coming to examine you and let you know what to expect. I'll make sure to be here before she arrives. I will call for the meal now."

The middle-aged woman who arrived the next morning was announced as the midwife. She examined Ara. "You are a healthy young woman. It is always difficult to tell for certain, but perhaps you only have two weeks before birth." She looked around her. "I see the priest has assigned all sorts of amulets to your apartment. The Church wants to give you every advantage." She didn't mention the number of babies and mothers she had seen die in childbirth.

"Not getting out of bed until after this baby is born is a terribly long time," remarked Aunt Clare.

"Let us say that Queen Ara needs to be in bed most of the time. She can get up to relieve herself, and she can walk around a little. She can also sit in a chair. Remaining in bed all the time isn't necessary." The midwife pulled up a chair near

Ara and leaned forward. "Don't let any of the noblewomen see you up," she warned. "They will be here to serve you, but they will act as a spy on you, as well."

"I know nothing about labor," confessed Ara. "How will I know when it begins?"

"Each woman is different. For some it is cramping in the belly, and for others it is pain and pressure in the back. Labor usually starts mildly and then intensifies over time. You will have plenty of time to be moved to the birthing room."

"Birthing room?" asked the three women together.

The midwife tried to act nonchalant, but she was uncomfortable. She shifted in her chair and addressed Ara. "Your Majesty, if you have a boy, you will give birth to the heir to the throne. It is important to the king and to the kingdom that it is known, with no doubt, that the child emerges from your body. Many courtiers will be watching you give birth."

"Men? There will be men watching me when I am exposed?" Ara sat up and howled. "I will be writhing in pain with my nightgown lifted for all to see? Tell me this isn't true!" Frieda and her mother exchanged glances. How horrible it will be for Ara.

"I am sorry, but it is so," replied the midwife.

"How many men? Who will they be?" Ara covered her face with the bedsheet.

"The doctor will be there, of course, and the Chancellor. In truth, any nobleman who cares to be a witness may attend.

Your aunt and cousin," the midwife glanced over at them, "will be present as well as a number of noblewoman. It is possible to have more than fifty people in the birthing room with you. Maybe more."

Ara began to breathe rapidly. "Oh, my goodness! How would I ever be able to show my face again once I have shown my... my netherparts?"

Aunt Clare leaned over her niece to give comfort. "You will hold your head up. You will have done nothing shameful. It is an honor to give birth and become a mother. Frieda and I will be with you. Just keep your focus on the baby."

Ara was not yet ready to be comforted. She turned away from the others and cried into her pillow. "Let us go into the other room," whispered Frieda. "She has been told much this morning and needs time to accept it." The three woman removed themselves from the room, and left Ara alone in her bed.

The weeks dragged by. Ara received a letter from the king wishing her well, but mentioned nothing about returning. She had come to accept the relationship, or lack of one, they had. Lady Belstrum visited with her every day. She sang songs for her and played the guitar. She fussed over her, too, smoothing her bedding, and combing her hair. Lady Belstrum inwardly shivered at the thought of the display Ara was facing. "I will be there with you," she promised, "and I will position myself to shield you as much as possible." Ara squeezed her hand in gratitude.

Other ladies came to attend her as well. They told riddles, played music for her, and some knitted alongside her. The lying-in was not as dreary as Ara had feared. Aunt Clare rose early to open the bedchamber window so Jana could enter each morning. Frieda had laughed at her mother's first reaction to the bird. It took days before Aunt Clare would venture near him. She was shocked when she learned that Jana had always been with her niece, but Ara never mentioned to either her cousin or her aunt that he had been her mother's friend first. She didn't want to explain it. It was too private.

CHAPTER 18

It was mid-afternoon when the cramping started. The contractions were mild, but frequent. *Could this be labor?* Ara thought. *If so, I can handle this pain.* She was beginning her third week of lying-in. The room was stuffy and stale from the lack of fresh air. Aunt Clara and Frieda were in the antechamber sorting the clothes the noblewomen had embroidered.

Two ladies were with Ara telling riddles when they noticed her slight grimace. "Please call my aunt in," she said softly. One of the ladies jumped up and came quickly back with Aunt Clare. Frieda trailed behind. "Feel this." Ara put her aunt's hands on her belly and waited. Her aunt could feel the mild movement.

"That's a contraction." She kept her hands in place and was surprised when another followed quickly. She said to no one in particular, "Get the midwife," and both ladies hurried from the room. One went for the midwife, and the other went to notify the courtiers.

By the time the midwife arrived, the contractions were stronger. She examined Ara. "Time to go to the birthing room, Your Majesty." She helped Ara from the bed. "You have to walk a little way but we'll help you." The baby was low in the belly, positioned for travel out in the world, making it difficult for Ara to walk. Frieda and Aunt Clara carried her.

The birthing chamber was made dark and dimly lit to represent a womb. Few candles were scattered about the room. The windows were shuttered and hung with heavy red velvet draperies. When Ara entered, she reeled back and turned her head. There were thirty men and women already there. Their laughing and talking stopped upon Ara's arrival and watched her climb into bed. One stood on a table to get a better view. Someone put a crucifix in one of her hands and a rosary in the other. The room steadily filled until the number exceeded sixty observers. "Pigs," muttered the midwife. Ara closed her eyes and focused on her cousin and aunt's reassuring hands on her.

With a whoosh, her water broke. Ara had been told about the birthing process, but it still came as a surprise. She could hear exclamations from the crowd. It did not take long after that for the contractions to go deep, prolonged, and hard. She was awestruck by the intensity of the pain, but set her jaw and refused to utter a complaint. Her only thought, her mantra, was *Be a girl. Be a girl. Be a girl.*

Lady Belstrum was appalled by the behavior of the men. They were ogling the process and pressing forward. As promised, she stepped up to the end of the bed to shield Ara as much as possible. The midwife pitied Ara. She grabbed the birthing chair and helped her sit upon it. It would give Ara a measure of cover. She was not going to expose Ara's private parts to the men. Now the four women clustered around Ara with the midwife directly in front, giving her as much concealment as possible. "Stand aside," one of the men called out, but he was ignored.

Ara began panting and bearing down. "The head has emerged!" exclaimed the midwife. "One more push." Ara bore down again and the baby was born. "It's a boy!" shouted the midwife, and a huge cheer erupted from the crowd.

Ara cried, "No, no," and began moaning. The men were slapping each other on the back as if they had given birth themselves. The commotion was so great, only Frieda and Aunt Clare were aware of Ara's distress. The others attributed her sobs as a release from the ordeal of birth.

Ara was inconsolable when she was brought back to her bedchamber. She refused to see the baby she would soon have to give up to the man who had spun gold for her. Aunt Clare and Frieda shooed everyone out of the apartment. They were alarmed at her reaction. They knew her to be a sensible and kind person; her baby should have given her joy. Because King Richard was seldom at the castle, and he was, at best, indifferent to her, they thought Ara would give all her love to this singular being.

She refused to suckle the baby. "Bring in a wet nurse," Aunt Clare whispered to the midwife.

Ara lay numb for two days. She was as mute as a stone and turned away whenever her chamber door opened. Her mind was racing. *When the Spinner comes to take the child, I have no recourse but to die,* she thought. *I could never explain the disappearance of my son. Richard will want my head. Better that I kill myself first.*

She awoke on the third day with throbbing, hard breasts. Her milk had come in, and that natural act her body performed changed her. It told her that her duty was to her child. She did not know how long he would be with her, but she would love and care for him until she yielded him to the man who saved her life years before. She laughed hollowly, aware of the irony that he would be the person to cause her death now.

Ara slipped out of bed and opened the door to the antechamber. Frieda and Aunt Clare were huddled near each other talking quietly. They raised their heads in surprise when they saw Ara. "Please bring me my baby," she said.

The baby slept in a cradle by Ara's bed. When he fussed, she rushed to pick him up. Nursing was a contented time for her. *He needs me,"* she thought. *I will not abandon him again.* She was seated with the baby in the antechamber with Frieda and Aunt Clare. "Richard is to return any day now. He will want to show his son off to all his noblemen."

"Many of them are at the castle now," said Frieda. "They have been assembling here to greet him when he arrives. There are more cooks in the kitchen to keep up with the meals."

"Lord Chancellor Richtmann told me to expect the christening the day after Richard arrives." Ara bent her head to inhale the scent of her baby.

"Then your son will finally have a name," remarked Aunt Clare. "I've never known a baby to go without one for so long."

"Two weeks is a long time," acknowledged Ara. She removed her son from her breast and put him to her shoulder. "I am happy to call him my *liebling* for now. I hope Richard chooses a good name."

"If the baby's done eating, I will hold him for a while," offered Frieda. "You have to have something to eat yourself."

Ara handed him over and walked unsteadily to the trays of food on the table. Her hands shook as she chose a piece of cheese and ale and settled herself down again. The thought of losing her baby was constant. "Ara, you are nursing. You must have more than the little food on your plate. You are too thin and frail," admonished Aunt Clare.

"I am told that ale is good for nursing," protested Ara, "and right now, my stomach cannot hold any more food." The Spinner could show up at any time demanding his payment. Her anger towards her father had risen again. *This is your fault!* she shouted at him inwardly. *I will lose my child and you will be the death of me.*

CHAPTER 19

King Richard arrived two days later, dusty from the road and ripe with the odor of a long ride on horseback. His stringy, unkempt hair matched the straggle of his russet beard. The three women were in Ara's apartment when the door swung open and he strode in. Jumping up from the sudden intrusion, they curtsied when they saw it was the king. "Where is my son?" he demanded.

Ara rushed into her bedchamber and returned with the sleeping baby nestled in her arms. "Here he is." She held him up for the king to see.

Richard smiled broadly. "He has my red hair."

"Yes, he looks just like you. It is yet too early to know for sure, but I think his eyes will be two different colors, too, just like yours. Would you like to hold him?" she asked.

He took a step back and raised his hands. "No. He is too small for me yet." He turned to Ara, inspecting her. She was dressed in only a smock and kirtle and her dark hair hung down her back. "You look gaunt and are dressed like a peasant."

"I am still lying in, and am not prepared to visit with anyone," Ara replied. She turned away, unaccustomed to his presence after an absence of half a year.

"The christening will be tomorrow, and we will celebrate in the great hall. Alfred has arrived and will be his godfather. Have the child there at noon, and dress like the queen I made of you." The women curtsied as he left brusquely.

Aunt Clare took a deep breath to keep her anger from rising. King or not, he had no call to treat Ara sharply. She took the baby from Frieda and fussed with him before she felt calm enough to speak. Frieda bit her lips and walked out of the room, afraid her angry thoughts would slip out. "Well, the king has returned. Our liebling will have a name in the morrow. I hope it is a good, strong one."

Ara was immune to the king's unkindness. She had stopped caring about his treatment of her years ago. It was just a matter of time before the Spinner appeared, anyway. Nothing else was a concern for her.

"This chamber will be bright again soon," Ara spoke to Jana in the morning. "The tapestries will be gone, and the windows will be exposed once more. When you arrive tomorrow, you shall see the change." The bird hopped away from her to perch on the baby's cradle. He eyed the child with interest. The infant was sleeping placidly, but every once in a while he would purse his lips and his body would twitch. He had lost the splotchy skin of birth and was now both creamy and rosy. "He's a beautiful baby, but not mine to keep." She was silent for several minutes. "I must prepare for the christening. Today he will get a name."

Ara had been humiliated when the noblemen gawked at her during childbirth. She shook her head to erase the memory. She had asked the seamstresses to make her a gown for the christening, one that would make here look serene, as though she had been unruffled by their gaping eyes from a score of days ago.

"Frieda, I think this gown has a coolness to it. If I have to face all the people who came to gawp at me during childbirth, I wish to look as though it made not a whit of difference to me."

She had chosen a shimmery white silk kirtle. An embroidered forepart made of cloth-of-gold was tied around Ara's waist. Atop it, Frieda helped her slip into an ice blue satin gown. Matching cloth-of-gold sleeves were pinned at the shoulders. Her hair was braided into a bun and covered in a mesh snood appointed with pearls. A crown of diamonds and sapphires was set atop her head. "You look beautiful," her cousin said, and Ara would have believed her if she wasn't emaciated. Her eyes and cheeks were sunken, and there was a haunted look about her.

The long walk to the great hall marked the end of Ara's lying in. Aunt Clare carried the baby, striding silently alongside her niece through the twisting gray corridors and down narrow staircases. Frieda followed two steps behind aware of the shuffling sounds of their shoes on the stone floor.

Loud voices and laughter dimmed to a murmur rippling through the room as they appeared at the entrance. Chancellor Richtmann led them down the center of room to Richard, flanked by Alfred and a priest. Ara stopped in front of them holding the baby in her arms while Frieda and her mother moved off to the side.

The priest said a prayer over the child and anointed him with oil and water. "What name do you give your son?" he asked the king.

When Richard answered, "Phillip," Ara smiled. It was a strong name, one that once belonged to the king's grandfather. A good choice was made. Alfred took the baby and holding him high in the air, he turned to the gathering. "I present to you Prince Phillip, the next king of the realm," he bellowed. The nobles bowed and curtsied.

The shout startled Phillip who began to wail. "Get him out of here," he snapped at Ara. Alfred placed the baby in her arms, and she turned to leave, but Richard stopped her. "You stay with me." She handed her son to Aunt Clare who quickly withdrew from the room with Frieda. Ara remained for the celebration.

By the time Ara returned to her apartment, she was frantic. Phillip was yowling with hunger. Aunt Clare was pacing the room with him in her arms, trying to get him to settle when Ara rushed in. "Get me out of these clothes so I can feed him," she begged Frieda while starting to unlace the gown herself. She was as distressed as her son. Her breasts were spilling milk as she took him into her arms. Only when Phillip began suckling were they both able to quiet themselves.

Richard visited Ara the next day. "Let's sit here," he said leading her to a settee. "I am leaving soon to go back north with my knights and soldiers." He paused. "To bring forth my son was a hard task. My courtiers said you uttered not one sound while they've heard other women cry out in pain during childbirth." Ara bowed her head remembering the agony and embarrassment of such a public labor.

"This is a birthing gift. It belonged to my mother." He handed her a purple velvet box. Ara opened it hesitantly. It had been a long time since Richard displayed a kindness to her. She was momentarily wary that a cruelty would be contained within. To her surprise, nestled inside was an exquisite round brooch encircled with diamonds. Ara lifted it out and Richard took it from her. "See, it opens here." He pressed a latch and the center popped open. "You can put something within it." He handed it back to her.

"It's a lovely gift." Ara was genuinely grateful. "When it is long enough, I will cut a lock of Phillip's hair and place it inside."

Richard slapped his knees and stood, the tender moment broken. "Then I am off to gather supplies. I will say farewell before I go. By the by, Alfred and Clotilde have brought a nursemaid for Phillip. The woman was employed by them when their sons were young. Clotilde will bring her to you later today." As swiftly as he came into the antechamber, he left leaving her still holding the brooch.

The sun had long passed its zenith by the time Alfred's wife visited, trailed by a sturdy, thick waisted woman in a simple gray gown and coif. Both of them curtsied to Ara. "This is a beautiful antechamber," said Clotilde as her eyes roamed the room. This must be a far cry from what your home at the mill was like."

"It is, indeed," Ara replied ignoring the cattiness in her guest's voice. "This room alone is nearly as large as my cottage in Belstrumburg, but that is where my mother lived, so it was even more special than this." She stared steadily at the princess, daring her to make another comment. The moment passed. "Please won't you both sit for awhile with me? I will send for refreshments."

"Thank you," Clotilde responded, inwardly balking at sharing a meal with her servant. She perched delicately upon a chair while the other woman sat fully into hers. "I wish to present Katerina. For years she has served as my children's nursemaid, and her mother was my nursemaid. She is dedicated to our family and I expect that she will oversee Phillip carefully."

A servant silently treaded into the room and lay a tray of meats and cheeses onto the table. Ara filled a plate and handed it to Katerina. "Right now I am watching over Phillip full time. On the occasions that I am unavailable, my Aunt Clara has been acting as nursemaid. She will be leaving soon, and then you will begin your full time duties. Meanwhile, observe the routine and begin slipping into the role. By the time my aunt leaves, the transition will be complete."

"That is a good plan," remarked Clotilde, picking a crumb from her lap. "Katerina will remain in our employ. That is to say that Alfred and I may wish her to return to us at some later date. She is our gift to you, and we will pay her salary."

"Is this a custom in royal life?" puzzled Ara.

"No, but I have known her all her life and am fond of her." She smiled at Katerina. "It is merely a kind gesture on Alfred's and my part to give Phillip the best nursemaid we know."

"How very thoughtful of you." Ara faced Katerina. "You are lucky, indeed, to have such a strong bond with the princess' family. I will make sure you have a warm bed and are well taken care of here."

Clotilde rose. "I will say goodbye to you now. You have assured me that Katerina will have a good stay here for as long as she is needed."

Ara walked them to the door. "My aunt will see to it that Katerina is well settled in the nursery."

Clotilde bowed to Ara. "This should work out perfectly."

It was a week before Ara realized Richard had departed the castle without saying goodbye to her. *He never asked to see the baby again*, she mused.

CHAPTER 20

By the time Phillip was six weeks old, Ara was beginning to feel hopeful. "Jana, the Spinner has not yet come," she whispered to the raven. The sun was streaming through the window, placing a rectangle of light on the chamber floor. "Maybe he is ill or has died." When food was brought to her, she was able to eat a little more.

It was time to say goodbye to Aunt Clare. "When Uncle Jasper is ready, come here to live. The king will take him on as the cooper." Ara sobbed in her aunt's arms. "I will miss you so." Aunt Clare began crying, too, as was Frieda who embraced her next.

"We will all miss you, Mama." She wiped tears from her eyes, and kissed her mother tenderly.

"I will bring Papa next time," Aunt Clare promised, as she settled herself into the carriage. "Goodbye, my darlings." Ara and Frieda stood arm in arm as they watched her carriage ride through the portcullis. Sighing, they returned to the apartment.

Their life together was simple. The afternoon midsummer sun was piercing, so they walked the gardens early each morning, taking turns carrying Phillip. Ara was regaining her strength, but didn't yet walk to the forest. She did, however, direct the landscapers to create a woodland garden full of shade plants including hostas, ferns, and colorful caladiums amid the paths along with secret fairy houses.

Mannus and Marie resumed their weekly visits with Ara, Frieda, and Hans. It was a lively group who told Ara stories to make her laugh. Their world was larger than hers, and they shared it with her as best as they could. Mannus and Marie gave her and Frieda riding lessons. Ara was comfortable around the horses, but had never been on the back of one before. Marie found the gentlest of the creatures, and soon Ara could canter side-saddle through the meadow. She felt free as her horse sliced the air. On those idyllic days, she, Frieda, and Marie would spread a blanket and eat a midday meal as the bees buzzed around them. It was the most contented time of her life since she was a child.

A year passed before Ara stopped thinking about the Spinner. Her son was weaned and she resumed attending the spinners and weavers groups. The women were delighted to see her and show their skills off to her. Occasionally she brought Phillip with her, and the women fussed over him. The women agreed he looked much like the king did when he was young. "It is a rare occurrence to have red hair with one eye blue and the other green. The king's great-grandmother, Queen Orla, was from the Gaelic Island and had such a combination. It was through her that our royals began carrying such a trait," commented the oldest spinner as she bounced him on her knee. "Besides the king and our little prince here, I know no one else like that. Surely, this is a sign of royalty."

Ara spent many hours spinning alongside them, smiling contentedly as the women chatted amongst themselves. Her mother's spinning wheel was smooth and shiny with age, whirring a tune she remembered from her youth. When she closed her eyes, she could see herself as a little girl feeling the first strands of flax turning into linen through her fingers.

The king returned victorious in his conquests to the north. "The people there are stubborn folk, and the land was hard to wrest from them." Richard was sitting in a winged chair in his solar. "Battles were fierce." Ara believed him. His arm was bandaged beneath his jacket having been badly sliced by a sword. A fever from the wound had developed, worrying him that it would need to be amputated. It had taken months before he could travel back to the castle. "Some kings don't go into battle, but I am not one of them. I have no respect for the ones who lead their men from behind. They are cowards. I captured the ones who fought with their knights and demanded their liege before setting them free. The others? I took their heads and delivered them to their castles." He laughed scornfully.

Phillip was tottering around, inquisitive about his new setting. Richard watched him, bemused. "He is now past his first birthday. Look how strong and smart he is. He will be fighting next to me one day."

A shiver ran through Ara. She wished she could scoop her son up and run away with him back to Belstrumburg. "By then you will have conquered all the lands you want, and he can be a benevolent prince at your side." She smiled nervously. Her strength had returned. The only one she feared now was her husband who was, by turns, affectionate and hostile.

"Nonsense," Richard replied. "There is a whole world out there to conquer, and with your ability to spin straw into gold, my revenues are unlimited." He took a long drink of mead. "You were quite a find, my dear." Richard looked at his wife steadily. Her face had filled out again and her color had returned to its rosy hue, although a hint of anxiety still showed on her face. He was pleased to see the diamond brooch he gave her pinned on her gown. "Call the nurse for Phillip. Stay with me tonight." It was not a request.

Before Richard returned to his wars to the north, he visited the treasury to examine his stores of gold. Ara had provided him with three rooms full of ingots. In these past six years, one was nearly depleted. He would have to empty it and draw from the second to resupply his men and build ships.

CHAPTER 21

Frieda put on her cloak and grabbed her gloves. Winter's icy weather was fast approaching. "I will see you tomorrow morning. Make sure the fire in the fireplace is properly stoked. It is getting chillier with each passing day."

Ara had just returned from the nursery. "The carriage will be waiting for you. I instructed the driver to put warm stones in it to keep you cozy. Hans will not want a cold wife."

Frieda grinned. "Hans never has a cold wife."

Ara kissed her cousin. "You can sleep in tomorrow, if you like. Phillip's nursemaid will feed and dress him."

"Katerina takes good care of Phillip. Stay in bed until I get here tomorrow. We'll go get Phillip together."

"I'll try, but Jana will be pecking at the window early enough."

After Frieda slipped out the door, Ara picked up her sketch book and sat at the fireside table. She was using charcoal to draw a portrait of Phillip. She picked up a piece of bread by her side to soften edges in the drawing. She was intent at her work, when, from the corner of her eye, she spied a shadow. She glanced up. Standing by the fire was the Spinner.

The bent and withered man was dressed as before in hunting garb. He held his hat with both hands. "I have come for the child, Ara." His gravely voice was low.

She jumped up, dropping her charcoal to the table. "No!" she cried. "I did not think you would come."

He shook his head. "I waited for Phillip to be weaned. I can care for him on my own now."

The Spinner had been watching. He knew her child's name. Ara's heart was pounding as she begged. "Please don't take my baby. He is my sun, my moon, my song. I will give you a castle, gold, jewels, cattle, anything you want."

"I do not need those things. I can spin straw into gold. You cannot give me anything I cannot provide myself."

"Except a child," whispered Ara.

The Spinner spoke softly. "We made a bargain long ago. I saved your life."

Ara burst into sobs, tearing at her hair and clothes. She had made the bargain years ago to save her life. Phillip was her greatest source of love and joy. He would not exist without the help of this wizened man, but how could she have known how steep a price it was to pay? "I beg of you, sir, do not take my child. I will surely die if you do." Dropping to her knees and pleading, she clasped her hands towards him. "He is my life. Please...please, do not take my son." She collapsed to the floor, her shoulders rising and falling as she weeped.

Tears welled in his eyes. He stepped to her and touched her arm. "We will make another bargain. You have three days to guess my name. If you do, you may keep your child. But if you do not, I will take him on the third day. I will be here tomorrow at sunset."

When Ara lifted her head, he was gone. As quickly and as silently as he had come, he had disappeared. She wiped her eyes, leaving streaks of tears and charcoal soot. There was hope, a chance to keep Phillip. She only needed to speak the Spinner's name. It would not be impossible. She pulled out another sheet of paper and began furiously writing down names with her charcoal. She was still at work when Jana pecked at her window in the morning. She wiped her hands on her nightgown as she let him in. "Ara! Ara!" he called, alarmed at the sight of her. He flew to the other side of the room.

Frieda dropped her gloves when she walked into the apartment the next morning as a distraught Ara ran to her with eyes red and glazed from lack of sleep. "Help me! I need to write down as many names as possible." Her voice was pitched high with panic. Her face was streaked black from a mingling of charcoal and tears.

"Calm down, Cousin. What has happened?" Frieda pulled Ara to a chair, but Ara jumped up and paced.

"I need names. Go amongst the servants and collect their names and...and...and their families' names. Bring Mannus to me. Now! I must sit here and write names."

"Why do you need names?" entreated Frieda frightened by Ara's frantic demeanor .

Ara rebuffed her. "I cannot tell you why. Go!"

Alarmed, she ran from the room to get Mannus. As they entered, Ara was pounding the table. "I cannot think of any more names," she muttered repeatedly. When she turned to them, Mannus was startled by her agitated state. Her nightgown and face were covered in charcoal, and her tangled hair fell into her face. He grabbled her by the shoulders and hugged her tightly.

"What is wrong, Ara?" he entreated.

Her chest heaved as she gulped for air. "Do not ask me. Gather your hunters and hunt not for animals, but for names. Go into the towns and villages. Write down the names of everyone, peasant, merchant, noblemen, and return them to me. Every name. It does not matter how strange or ordinary it is. I need a list of names."

"I will do this, but it will take a week or more to collect them."

"I need them no later than three days. It will be too late after that." Ara's eyes darted between Frieda to Mannus. "Please help me."

"I will go now," said Mannus. "I will get some of the grooms to help, too." He kissed her cheek. "Do not fret. We will be back in time."

Frieda caught him by the arm as he turned to go. "I'm told there are a few families and hermits who live in the woods. Get their names, too." Mannus nodded and hurried from the room.

Ara was pacing back and forth, wringing a handkerchief. Frieda led her to the bathroom. "I am going to clean you up. You'll be able to think better when you are washed. Then you are going to get your son. Focus on him and I will gather names."

Frieda tenderly sponged Ara who became very still, staring blankly. Numbly Ara allowed herself to be dressed and sat silently as Frieda combed her hair. "Do you want to tell me now what is the matter?"

"I cannot. It would be a danger for you to know. Do not ask me again." Ara's voice was emotionless.

"You need to go see Philip. He will be waiting for you. I will go to the staff and collect names."

"Yes," replied Ara distractedly. Then she looked at Frieda. "You are my steady companion and my dearest friend. I will depend on you to get me names. You must return before sunset." Ara brought Frieda's hands to her lips and kissed them. Then she swiftly left the apartment to get Phillip.

CHAPTER 22

Ara watched Frieda's carriage drive out of the castle grounds. In her hand were long lists of names. The candles flickered as she hurried through the twisting corridors to her apartment, and then sat motionless waiting for the Spinner. Precisely at sundown, he stood quietly before her, appearing first as a shimmer before becoming fully formed.

"Good evening, Ara," he spoke just above a whisper. "Do you know my name?"

She began with all the familiar ones. "Is it Spinner?"

"No."

"Hans."

"No."

"Mannus?"

"No."

"Richard?"

"No."

Jasper?"

"No."

"Klaus?"

Ara spoke each name on the list clearly. She did not lift her eyes from the papers. The Spinner stood motionless all the while, blinking only occasionally as he replied no to each name. She finished her lists hours after she had begun. With a deep sigh, she let the papers slip from her hands and pinched her brow.

"I will return again tomorrow at sundown." He bowed and disappeared.

Ara's stomach lurched and she vomited onto the wooden floor. She had only two more days to find his name. *I cannot fail,* she thought. *I must not fail.*

Frieda arrived early the next morning, carrying a tray of hot food. Ara was already at the writing desk with Jana who was rubbing his beak against her cheek. "You must eat," Frieda insisted, setting it on a table. "You look haggard. Did you sleep? You are still in yesterday's clothes."

"I was too anxious to sleep. Look," Ara pointed to the book laying on her desk. "I went to the library and found this French book. I am writing down all the names in it."

"Eat something and I will go with you back to the library to look for more names."

The two women spent hours searching through foreign language books. They pulled down astronomical tomes from the shelves and wrote down the names of the planets and stars. They wrote the colors of the rainbow. Finally, they rubbed their eyes and stretched their backs. "I will go search out any returning hunters and get their lists. You need to spend some time with Phillip," said Frieda.

Wearily Ara pushed back her chair. "You are right." A conflict was raging within her. The hours she was using to look for names were taking precious time from her son. If she did not say the Spinner's name, she would forever regret not spending those last hours with him.

By late afternoon, some of the hunters and grooms returned with lists of names. Frieda compiled them with hers and had them waiting for her cousin when she reentered her chambers. Ara grabbed at the papers and scanned them. Some of them were repeats of names she had said before, but there were many new ones. "Marie helped, too," acknowledged Frieda "She gave me a list of birds, mammals, fish, amphibians, and reptiles." She handed Ara two more sheets. "This one has the names of all the Greek and Roman gods and goddesses, and the last one is filled with plant names."

Ara slumped into a chair and closed her eyes. She twitched silently for several minutes. Her movements reminded Frieda of a butterfly inside a chrysalis. Finally, her back straightened and her eyes opened. "These are good lists." She stood up, rustling her skirts. "It's nearly six. Hans will be waiting for you."

"Let me stay with you," implored Frieda.

Ara shook her head. "No, I must be alone. Go to your husband, quickly now. It's late." She gathered her cousin's cloak and hat and kissed both of her cheeks. "I will see you in the morrow." Firmly Ara escorted Frieda to the door and latched it after her. She gathered up the lists to wait for the Spinner. Looking over the lists once more, she felt the texture of the papers. They were made of linen.

She didn't wait long for the Spinner to appear. "Good evening, Ara," he said, repeating his greeting from the night before. His bent body was rigid as he stood before her. "Do you know my name?"

"Jacques?"

"No."

"Pierre?"

"No."

Ara went through the list of foreign names and on to animals, then plants, and gods. She called out the colors and names of the townspeople. With every guess, the Spinner replied no.

The candles burned down, and the stars crossed the sky by the time Ara finished the lists. For the first time since she began reading, she looked at this strange man who had saved her life years ago. "I am trying to keep my son." Her bottom lip trembled.

"I know you are, Ara. You have one more night yet." His raspy voice was gentle. "I will see you tomorrow." His body shimmered as he faded away.

The raven flew down from the window. "Jana!" He flew around the room and nestled in her lap. She raised him up to her face. "Did you see that man? Can you find where he

lives?" Jana shook his feathers and spread his wings. "Love
Ara," he called and flew off into the night.

Sitting once again at the desk, she picked up the quill, but
hadn't the strength to write. She hadn't meant to sleep, but
her body was worry weary. It was only when Frieda gently
shook her the next morning that she knew she had slumbered.
She was momentarily bewildered and shielded her eyes from
the light.

"Come you, get up," ordered Frieda. "A warm bath is
waiting for you, and I have a fresh gown." She held Ara up by
the waist and half dragged her to the tub, but Ara was too weak
to climb in. "I'm going to call the doctor," worried Frieda.

"No, please, I don't want to see anyone."

"Then let me help you." Frieda was firm but worried.
She cleaned and dressed her cousin and placed her at a table.
Ara sat limply, hanging her head. "If you don't gather your
strength, I cannot let Phillip see you in this state."

"I must see my son," she implored. Frieda's words stirred
her. She shook herself. This may be the last day she would be
with him. "I will eat and then go to him."

Frieda watched Ara break her fast. She wasn't sure if it was
her words or the food that revived her cousin, but Ara seemed
refreshed. It was only when she fumbled the door latch that
she belied her weakness.

Mannus found his sister waiting for him when he galloped
into the stables in the afternoon. Jumping off the horse, he
took out the lists from his deerskin purse. Handing them to

Frieda he said, "These are all the names the men and I could find. Most are ordinary names but there are a few strange ones. Have you found out why Ara needs them?"

"I do not know, but she is terribly frightened. I have never seen her in such a panic."

She looked over the lists. There were only a few new names. "Have all the men come back?"

"Only Manfred is out yet. I will get you his names as soon as he arrives."

"Pray that it is soon. Ara refuses to see me past sundown." Frieda left her brother to unsaddle his horse while she brought the lists to Ara who scanned them. She was sure she had read most of the names aloud already, but she only needed one to keep her child. Maybe it was one of the new ones. She put her hopes there.

A sharp knock on the door brought both women to their feet. Mannus strode into the room followed by another man who bowed low. "This is Manfred. He has just come from deep within the woods and has a story."

"Beg pardon, Your Majesty. I was out riding in the forest looking for hermits, but I saw no one. Out from nowhere a raven dove at me. I took out an arrow to shoot it, but it flew away. I chased after it, it attacked me again, knocking off my cap. Once more I pursued it, but it was quickly out of range. I thought it was gone for good when the rascal hit me from behind. I was angry and determined to kill it, but it kept flying from tree to tree. Just as I was aiming, I heard a voice from beyond the brambles. It was a small man busy stirring a pot of stew and singing a strange song."

"Go on," encouraged Ara. "Tell me the song."

"I have long lived alone
With no babe to call my own
To love and hold and cradle near
To watch him sleep and call him dear.
But soon Ara's child I'll claim
For Rumpelstiltskin is my name."

"Oh," gasped Ara. "Are you sure? Rumple...Rumple what?"

"Rumpelstiltskin," replied the hunter. "I am sure. I repeated this song all the way back here."

Ara rushed to the desk to write the name down. "Thank you, sir. If this is the correct name, you shall be rewarded." She turned to the three of them. "You must leave me. The time is getting late." For the first time in days she sounded hopeful.

Once again she waited in silence, only this time her heart was lighter. Within a blink, the Spinner stood before her. "Good evening, Ara. Do you know my name?"

Before her was the man who saved her life, the one who wanted nothing more than a child. He could have taken Phillip according to the bargain they made, yet he had given her another chance to keep him. She knew, by speaking his name, his chance at a family would be gone.

"I have a list of names here," Ara began, "but I do not think I need it." She thought she saw him quiver.

"Go on. Say my name." He planted his feet and squared his shoulders as if he expected a physical blow.

"Rumpelstiltskin."

The room began to shake and a howl filled the air. It was long and deep and despairing. Ara watched him disappear into a vapor. He left a puddle that she understood were his tears. She wept because she could keep Phillip, and because her savior had given up his chance to have a son.

CHAPTER 23

At last Ara felt free. Jana had discovered Rumpelstiltskin and led the huntsman to him. Without her bird, she would never have guessed Rumpelstiltskin's name. Now she was released from the fear of losing her son. Richard had been away for over a year conquering lands in his quest for an empire, and she was free of her fear of him, at least for the time being.

There was a lightness about Ara, one that had been missing since the death of her mother, a millstone lifted from her chest. At last she breathed the clean, fresh air of happiness. Her smile was broad, and her face once again filled with a healthy glow. Her footsteps were as light as butterfly wings.

Frieda was amazed at the change of her cousin. She could not guess at what had caused Ara's distress one month ago nor her sudden release from it. Whatever the reason, she was pleased to see genuine pleasure show in the whole of Ara's being.

The two women were walking arm in arm from the stables after an afternoon of riding, heading for the gardens. High, scudding clouds caused the sun to flicker. They paused by Peter's grave. Ara bent down and pulled the few weeds near his headstone, and then straightened her spine. "I have an idea," she said, her eyes brightening. "Let's go back to Belstrumburg for a short stay. I haven't returned since I left seven years ago. What do you say? Hans has never been there."

Frieda smiled broadly. She had only returned once since she left home. "I would love to show Hans our little village. When would you like to go?"

"Perhaps next week. Let me make arrangements to stay with Lord and Lady Belstrum. We'll take just a four day trip, including the two days travel back and forth."

"Will it be hard for little Phillip? He gets sick riding in a carriage."

"That is so." Ara paused. "I could leave him with Katerina. She has been encouraging me to let him spend more time with her."

"Then the matter is settled. Hans and I will stay with my parents. You should, too. They will want you there."

"I fear that your parents will then be bothered by some of the villagers. They will see me more as the queen than simply Ara, the miller's daughter. It will be easier if I stay up at the manor house. Besides, if Mannus and Marie come, too, there will be no room for me."

"Maybe Mannus will come, but I doubt if Marie will. Her baby is due in two months, and the trip would be uncomfortable for her."

Located below ground level, the kitchen was reached through a small wooden door and down a set of stairs. The cook and undercooks were busy preparing the evening meal for the men-at-arms who guarded the castle and the domestic servants. The heavy scent of meat pies and beef stew filled the room. Loaves of bread fresh from the oven lined a side table. Earthenware jugs stood on wooden shelves in a side alcove while baskets of onions and turnips sat ready to be chopped for the stew. Hanging from a beam within easy reach were twined bunches of dried herbs, rosemary, parsley, and sage, among them. The staff stopped their work to curtsy when Ara and Frieda entered. "Good afternoon, Your Majesty," they called out in unison.

"Good afternoon," replied Ara. "It smells heavenly in here." She peeked into a huge pot resting on a base in the fireplace. Hot coals had been set below to keep the stew bubbling.

"Would you and Lady Frieda like a bowl?" asked the cook. "The meat is tender now."

"Thank you, no," replied Ara, "but could we dip a bit of bread into the stew?"

"Surely." The cook broke off two pieces of brown bread and handed one to each of them.

Frieda and Ara dipped their bread and took a bite. "Delicious," savored Ara. They bid the staff goodbye and took the narrow staircase up to the great hall, silent without the king or courtiers. Their footsteps echoed as they walked across the floor to another set of stairs.

When they neared the nursery, they raced to the door, laughing. Frieda reached it first and entered. Phillip was on the rug with blocks scattered around him. Katerina slumped on a chair nearby looking slightly bored. She sat up at the sound of the opening door. "Mama!" cried Phillip as Ara scooped him into her arms. She covered his face and neck with kisses.

"Katerina, you can have the remainder of the day off, if you like," she offered. "Lady Frieda and I will stay with him. I'll keep him in my room tonight, so you won't be needed until the morning."

The nursemaid curtsied. "Thank you, Ma'am." She quickly withdrew from the room.

Phillip reached for Frieda who twirled him around before setting him down. They spent the afternoon with him in the nursery building towers with blocks and watched him laugh as he knocked them down. Later they gathered his nightclothes and brought him to Ara's chambers.

"I am going home to Hans tonight. Tomorrow when Mannus and Marie come here for supper, we'll make plans for our trip. But first," Frieda laughed, "I am stopping in the kitchen for some of the stew. I'll pack some up to take home for Hans and me. I will be back early tomorrow morning." She kissed Phillip and her cousin and left.

With hours of daylight remaining, Ara took Phillip out to the stables to look at the horses. Peacocks and chickens roamed about the stalls to the delight of her son. She let him pet her horse, and he watched her feed it an apple while he stood shyly behind her.

Jana flew overhead as they walked to the woods where she showed him some fairy houses the gardeners built into the trees. The sunlight was dappled and Phillip jumped in and out of the bright spots on the ground. Ara could hear Jana croaking in the branches. She stopped in front of a young, sturdy tree and lifted Phillip into her arms. "Do you see this oak tree? It is my favorite one. If you look carefully, there is a smiling face in the bark. Can you see it here?" She traced the outline of the eyes, nose, and grinning mouth, and he reached out to touch it. "The branches are low and they say hello to me whenever I walk by. Can you say hello to the tree?"

"Hello," Phillip laughed.

"This tree is your friend, too, and when you are tall enough, it will pat you as you walk by." Ara's eyes glistened when he hugged the tree.

"Mama's tree," he said. "My tree."

Yes, it's our tree. Wave goodbye to the tree. It's time to go back to the castle."

"Bye tree," called Phillip as he waved.

It was nearly dusk by the time they reached the castle. Back in her rooms Phillip was content to play with a small tin bird while Jana perched unobtrusively on the window sill. Ara sat quietly in a chair with her sketchbook and pencil drawing her son. Later, when he fell asleep in her arms, she placed him in a crib she kept by her bedside. In the morning, when he awoke, she could hear him babbling to himself. Maybe he was talking about the horse he saw yesterday or the walk in the woods. It was hard to say.

CHAPTER 24

The Saturday morning of the trip to Belstrumburg broke gray and dull, but Ara was cheerful. "Jana, I am returning home for a visit. You have probably been there many times over the years, haven't you?" When she picked him up and stroked him, a feather dropped from his wing. "I will take this with me. Will you stay here and watch over Phillip for me? Katerina is a good nurse, but I trust you the most." He croaked, "Ara, love Ara," which she took as a yes.

The trunk carrying Ara's clothes was loaded onto the carriage. She and Frieda had argued over the contents. Ara wanted to wear a simple smock and kirtle on her visit home, but Frieda was adamant that her cousin bring clothing that befit her station. "The people from the village are proud that you are queen. They will be disappointed if you come dressed looking like the rest of them."

"I am one of them. I will always be the miller's daughter from Belstrumburg. They will think that I think I am above them." They compromised with an elaborate gown for church and a simple outfit for the next day.

They clattered off in a carriage pulled by four horses. It had padded seats and sides, the most comfortable ride Ara ever had. Marie insisted that Mannus go, promising to stay with her parents until he returned. He sat with his cousin, holding her hand. She was anxious to see her old friends. Hans was happy for Frieda to return to her village, but since Ara had been little more than a captive in the castle for the past seven years, this trip was even more exciting for her. He and Frieda were keen to see the faces of the villagers when they saw the queen in mass on Sunday.

The foursome talked of Hans' merchandising business. Ara and Frieda were proud that he sold the linen from the guild. Over the years, his father began handling less of the business, giving more responsibility and income to his son. They chattered on about Mannus becoming a father, and how responsible a man he had become. They sang songs and told stories to occupy their time until the last hour of the trip. Then both women drew silent and contemplative about returning home.

The carriage ride was hours faster than the day-long trip Ara took to the castle in the work wagon nine years ago. She remembered little of the scenery of the trip other than the villages giving way to fields and forests. Mature trees graced both sides of the long driveway to the Belstrum manor forming a shaded arch. Ara had never seen the house or grounds up close before, only viewing them from a distance looking up the hillside. It was grander than she imagined as a child. There was a back wing she couldn't see from the mill, and formal gardens on one side. Servants had seen them coming up the long drive and were standing at attention when the carriage stopped at the manor door.

The butler stepped up and opened the carriage door. Ara emerged last, taking the butler's gloved hand while the entire staff bowed and curtsied to her. The party was led into the house, past the great hall to a receiving room where the Lord and Lady of the manor greeted the party warmly. "We are honored that you are staying with us. We have some refreshments ready and have chambers prepared for all of you. You can rest before supper tonight."

"Thank you, my Lord, but my sister, her husband and I will stay with my parents," replied Mannus. "We beg your pardon, but we would like to be with with them."

Lord Belstrum nodded. "Certainly. Since you want Ara's visit to be a surprise, we will ready a simple wagon for your ride to your parents' cottage. It won't raise the interest of the villagers," he said. "Have a small repast and I will have the wagon prepared."

They sat chatting amicably, drinking wine, and eating a light meal. The room was bright as the late afternoon sun slanted in. Paintings of horses and bucolic scenes filled the walls, and tall, heavy, oak cabinets stood on either side of the fireplace. Oriental rugs were scattered on the floor.

A knock at the door let them know the wagon was ready. After thanking the Belstrums for their hospitality, Frieda turned to Ara. "We will see you in church tomorrow. Wear the gown," she reminded her. "Everyone will want you to look like their queen."

After her three companions left, Ara and the Belstrums had a lengthy visit, until she stifled a yawn. Despite her weariness from travel, Lady Belstrum could see a contented Ara. She was less reserved and smiled more. Something had happened to make Ara happier. Perhaps it was the long separation from the king or that childbearing was over. Whatever it was, Ara was more enlivened and talkative.

It was late when Ara was led to her bedchamber. Gilded leather covered the walls that arched up to meet the ceiling. Fresh flowers sat on the table next to the canopied bed. Lady Belstrum sent in her lady's maid to help Ara prepare for bed. Once alone, she inhaled the gentle scent of lavender that permeated the sheets. Closing her eyes, she fell into a dreamless sleep.

Katerina took the small rock from her trunk that Princess Clotilde had given her before she departed the castle last year. You will know when it is a good time to use it, she had said. It will be best for the kingdom. Now, thought Katerina, was the time. She only had to work up her courage. She looked at Phillip sleeping peacefully in his crib. He was an easy child to care for, inquisitive and friendly, loving even. She wasn't sure she could carry out the deed.

CHAPTER 25

Lady Belstrum helped her maid dress Ara for church. Her red satin gown was embroidered with gold threads running down the placket and the sleeves. Her kirtle underneath showed rubies and pearls along the neckline. Encircling her waist was a belt of garnets. Ara's chestnut hair was covered by a bejeweled hood. "You looked beautiful," smiled Lady Belstrum. "The perfect queen."

Ara blushed. "I am the little girl searching for a whale that my father told me was swimming up the river."

"You are both. Let us go. We must time our arrival to be last in church. My husband has gone ahead to whisper our surprise to the priest. You are sure to disrupt mass." She laughed.

The driver held the coach back a distance from the church. Ara watched as friends excitedly greeted Mannus and Frieda. It pleased her to see her cousins embraced by old companions. Frieda's warm and amiable personality naturally attracted people to her. When all the congregants were inside the church, the carriage moved forward. Lord Belstrum helped the women out. He reviewed the plan. "My wife and I will enter first. Wait until we are seated, and then walk down the aisle. The priest expects the disruption and will keep the mass short. Enjoy the moment."

Ara stood at the back of the church and waited. The scent of old incense and melted wax mixed with the smell of sweating bodies. The nostalgia overwhelmed her and tears welled, threatening to spill down her cheeks. She caught the eye of the priest who motioned her forward. Inhaling deeply, she began her walk. The congregation was facing forward and it was only when she had taken several steps did they realize she was there. They began applauding and calling out her name. People stood and began crying. Ara laughed looking at the familiar faces of her youth. She grabbed Frieda's hand and squeezed it as she sat down. She heard not a word of the mass.

A receiving line was formed outside the church after the mass ended. Ara was as anxious to greet everyone from the village as they were to greet her. Klaus Becker was among the first in line. "You look beautiful, Ara," he said. "I brag to people that I escorted the queen to the fair."

"And a wonderful day it was," she replied. He presented his wife to her, and Ara clasped her hand warmly. "You are lucky to be married to so fine a man. You must be a special lady to be picked by him." Klaus blushed.

She hugged Mrs. Becker and Mrs. Weaver tightly. "You helped me during a dark period in my life. I will be eternally grateful to you." They both dabbed at their eyes.

"I didn't think I would ever see you again." Mrs. Weaver curtsied.

"I bow to both of you. I was a lost girl and there were the two of you. I didn't feel alone."

Mr. Kaufman was among the last in line. He stood silently in front of her and she grasped his gnarled hands. "You believed in me. You were my first customer."

"I blame myself for your mother's death." His shoulders sagged.

"Then you are wrong. It was an accident, nothing more."

He sobbed silently, and Ara took him in her arms and held him close. "Please do not suffer anymore. My mother would want you to have peace, as do I."

Together they walked out of church and she joined her cousins in the carriage. "I will do a walkabout tomorrow," she called out. "I will see you then." She waved as the coach rolled away. When they arrived at the Cooper household, she jumped out and ran into her aunt's arms. "I have missed you so," she cried. She turned to Uncle Jasper who squeezed her tightly and kissed her forehead.

The group moved into the cottage and sat around the table in the cozy keeping room. Frieda helped her mother served breakfast. "I cannot wait until Marie has her baby and you come to stay at the castle again."

Aunt Clare smiled at her son. "I will come as soon as I get word. I do not want to step into Marie's mother's role. She will want to help her."

"Marie's mother has several children underfoot," said Mannus. "She won't be able to help as much as she would like. We will be grateful that you will be there for her."

Ara looked around the room. It was a comfortable space with a table sitting in the center and a spinning wheel nestled into the corner next to Uncle Jasper's chair. She remembered him sitting there companionably whittling while Aunt Clare spun and she, Frieda, and Mannus played jacks on the floor. The cottage always smelled of rosemary and sage, as it did now. She would forever be grateful to her aunt for embracing her into the family after her mother died, refining her basic cooking skills, and giving her the hugs her mother no longer could and her father wouldn't.

She glanced at Frieda who loved as fiercely and loyally as her mother. She was suddenly overcome with emotion, and turned her face away from the others. *How lucky I am to have this family. In my time of need, they took me in and loved me as one of them.* Frieda looked at her and grinned. It was a fine homecoming.

After breakfast, she, Frieda and Hans walked to her old home. Sig answered the knock on the door. "Ara!" he exclaimed, bowing. "I heard you were in church this morning. Please, come in." He opened the door wider and stepped aside.

"Thank you, no, Sig, but, please, can we go to the mill? I would like to see it again."

"Of course," he said, and the four of them walked the little way together. Hans had never been inside one before, and Sig explained all the mechanics of the place. He kept it in fine form.

"My father used to call it the Old Man because the ivy reminded him of a beard, and the roof used to sag. I see you fixed it."

"The mill is my pride."

"I can tell. There is no better person to be the miller than you."

Sig swelled with gratification. "It means a great deal to hear you say that. It has been in your family for generations. I hope it will be in mine, as well."

When they returned to the Cooper homestead, Frieda helped Ara change into her smock and kirtle. "This feels so much better. I can move about and be free."

"I have a surprise," announced Frieda. "While you were greeting everyone after mass, I arranged a picnic with all of our friends. We will meet in the meadow. Help me get some food together, and we'll grab a quilt and go."

Ara's face lit up. "Wonderful idea." They went downstairs to find Aunt Clare getting out baskets. "We will do the rest of this," she said. "You and Uncle Jasper should come with us."

"No, this is just for you young folk. Go enjoy yourselves."

Frieda and Ara packed up food in the baskets and headed out to the meadow with Mannus and Hans. Already some of their friends were there. When they saw Ara in her simple clothing, they relaxed. She was once again their friend and nothing more.

Ara and others began stamping about, trampling the long grass to make a large area for them to sit. It was what they did when they were young, holding hands and walking in a circle. When they were done, they spread quilts out on the ground and set the baskets in the corners. She pointed out the corncrake and meadow pipet to Hans who never experienced the joy of a meadow. She watched the dragonflies hover and fly backwards before speeding away. The bees were busy feeding on the wild strawberry flowers, and here and there were spiders crawling around looking for a meal. She and her friends reminisced about old times, playing at each other's houses, especially on lazy Sunday afternoons. They shared their food and beer, sitting back on their elbows allowing the sunshine to spill over them.

A lone black bird came into view, flying fast and diving low towards them. Mannus saw it first. "Ara, look!"

She jumped up as it began calling, "Ara, Ara, Ara!"

One of the young men yelled, "It's a crazy bird. Kill it!"

Mannus shouted, "Leave it alone. It's Ara's bird."

It flew to her and she caught Jana in her hands. He said one word, "Phillip."

Ara turned to her cousins, her voice panicky. "He has never said his name before. Something is wrong with my son. I have to get back to Lundgrin."

"I will get two horses and you and I will ride back together. They will be faster than a carriage." Mannus took off running back to the cottage with Ara, Frieda, and Hans close behind. Mannus ran over to the carriage driver and told him to get them back to the manor as fast as possible. He helped Ara into the coach and they took off, Mannus yelling instructions to Frieda. "Get back to the castle as soon as you can."

Mannus jumped out of the carriage before it came to a stop at the Belstrum manor and pounded on the door. He and Ara rushed in as soon as the door opened. They explained that she received a message to return to Lundgrin as soon as possible, and requested the fastest horses from the stables.

"I can ride as a man, not side saddle. I have done it many times. It will be faster for us," insisted Ara.

"We will get back as fast as we can, but we must moderate our speed," cautioned Mannus, "or our horses will collapse beneath us. Stay calm, Cousin. We can do nothing until we return, and we will get back faster if we do not overwork the horses."

Ara was trembling with fear for her son. She took deep breaths to calm herself. Lady Belstrum brought her a pair a men's breeches. "Put these under your smock and tie them to your waist. They will be too big, but your legs will get chafed if you do not wear them."

The horses were brought to the front of the house. Mannus helped Ara up into the saddle, and then climbed onto the other. "Thank you. We are off." With no more words to spare, they headed back to the castle.

They rode without speaking, Ara resisting galloping ahead, letting Mannus set the speed. She forced her mind to go blank, determined only to get back to her son. She focused on Jana flying ahead. He would wait in a tree until they approached and then would fly on. As the sun began to set, she tried willing it to stay in the sky, fearful of the difficulty of riding in the dark.

Hours passed. Sometimes Mannus ordered them to slow down. "Let us not weary the horses." Then they would pick up their speed again. When a gibbous moon rose, Ara gave a silent thanks. It would not be too dark, and they would have no trouble keeping to the road.

Finally, Ara spied Lundgrin Castle up ahead. She had not seen it from this vantage point in several years and was struck by the immense size of it. When she could stand it no larger, she spurred her horse and charged ahead, her cousin following close behind. She halted at the immense oaken door. Mannus jumped from his steed, and helped her down. Both ran into the castle taking the stairs two at a time.

She and Mannus ran across the great hall and up the flights of stairs. The nursery door had been splintered and ajar. A guard at the nursery door stepped aside as they bolted into the room. Ara was shocked to find both Chancellor Richtmann and Doctor Bergan with Phillip. She rushed to his bed, and looked at her unconscious son. Vomit was on his chin and shirt. Ara grabbed for her him, but the doctor stopped her. "Don't touch him. He's very sick. He can keep nothing inside him." He paused for a beat. "He was poisoned."

"Poisoned? Who would poison my son?" cried Ara.

"His nursemaid," answered Lord Richtmann.

"Katerina? That cannot be so. She was good to Phillip." Ara's eyes darted between the chancellor and the doctor.

"It is true. She put arsenic in his porridge."

"Will he get better? Tell me he will get better." Her fists clenched and unclenched.

The doctor did not want to leave Ara without hope. "There is a chance that he will, but Phillip is a sick boy. He needs a great deal of liquid. Come sit with your son while I administer to him." Mannus placed a chair by the bedside and eased Ara into it. She sat stone faced holding her son's small hand. It was hot.

Mannus led the chancellor into the hallway. "How do you know Katerina did it? Where is she now?"

The chancellor ran his fingers through his hair. "She's dead. Two servants heard her scream and watched her jump from the window. She was dead on impact. A lump of arsenic was found in her pouch around her waist. Her hands were covered with it, too. The servants recognized her and alerted the guards. When they got to the nursery, the door was locked. They needed to break down the door to get to the prince. There was no one else in the room."

"Katerina must have been horrified by what she did and killed herself," mused Mannus. "I can think of no other explanation. Say nothing to the queen. I will tell her later. Let her just be with her son for now."

Mannus stayed by Ara's side all night, quietly giving her the news about Katerina. The doctor kept watch on Phillip, administering liquids intermittently. By morning there was little change in Phillip. Food was brought up to the room. "You must eat, Ara," insisted Mannus. "You will be no good to your son if you are sick."

He brought her over to a settee and fed her some pottage and bread. "Let me rest against you, Mannus." He held her in his arms and the two of them closed their eyes, exhaustion overtaking them quickly.

Voices by the child's bed awakened them. Frieda and Hans were talking softly to the doctor. Ara got up slowly. The long horse ride jarred her body and her muscles cried out in protest as she moved. She slipped her arm around Frieda's waist. "The doctor said Phillip is making some improvement."

Ara looked at the doctor who nodded. "He may not have ingested as much as I feared. He's not vomiting or evacuating his bowels any longer, and his color is returning. Still, he is very fragile."

"I am so grateful you were here, Doctor," said Ara, letting out a long breath. "Normally you are not about the castle when the king is not here."

"It was a strange thing. I wasn't here. I was in my study at home, and I heard a voice urging me to go to Phillip. I don't believe in such nonsense as ghosts, but I felt compelled to check on your son.

"When I arrived, the nursery door had been broken and the prince was violently vomiting. I would never have thought of poisoning, but I heard that same voice whispering in my ear telling me to check for it.

"Then I learned that the nursemaid had killed herself and I had the guards look for arsenic on her, and they found a pure lump of it in her pouch. The doctor stared off. "If I believed in them, I would say that Phillip had a guardian angel." He shook his head. "This is as close to a miracle as I've ever seen."

"I want to hold him." The doctor nodded. Ara sat in the chair and he placed Phillip in her arms. She cradled her son, rocking him tenderly.

Mannus eyed the two of them. "I will come back later with Marie," he whispered to Frieda. She nodded and he slipped from the room.

By mid-afternoon, Phillip's eyes fluttered open. "Hello, little one," Ara said softly. He was still in her arms. He whimpered. "I have you. You are safe with me."

"Mama," he mouthed. His eyes closed and he slept. Ara placed him back in his bed. She lay next to him, too tired to dream. Frieda watched over both of them.

The sun had set by the time Phillip awoke again. Frieda helped Ara wash and dress him in fresh clothes. He was lying limply in his mother's arms when Mannus and Marie arrived. "He looks weak, but improved," he observed, stroking his forehead.

"The worst is over," Dr. Bergan announced after checking Phillip. "By the end of the week, he should be bouncing all over the room. Give him a little food several times a day. His stomach and bowels need time to recover."

Ara sat back and sighed with relief. She gently handed her son to Marie and walked the doctor to the nursery door. "That voice you heard...was it a man's voice or a woman's?"

He spoke slowly, studying the floor. "It was definitely a man's voice, low and raspy. I shall never forget it. Strange, I've never had anything like that happen before." He looked up, his demeanor heartened. "Your son will get well, my queen. I will return daily to look after him." He bowed and left.

Frieda made room for her at the table. "I need to thank all of you," began Ara. "Marie, thank you for insisting Mannus go back to Belstrumburg with us." She looked at Mannus. "I could never have ridden back on the horse without you. I wouldn't have had the nerve." She turned to Frieda. "As always, you knew what I needed. You let me go and took care of what remained behind."

A smile came to Frieda's lips. "I always try to do what is best for you, and what you need most now is a good soak in the tub. From that horse ride and the past few days holding Phillip, you stink!"

Ara drew back. "Do I?"

They all agreed. "Yes!"

"I already have a chambermaid ready with hot water," said Frieda. "I was going to push you into the tub if I had to."

"All right," she laughed. "I will go back to my apartment and have a bath." She rose and returned to her chambers. As she began stripping off her clothes, something shiny on the floor caught her eye. Stooping to pick it up, she realized it was her mother's gold wheat ring, the one she had given the Spinner many years ago. She slipped it on her finger. *So it was he who came to the aid of my son. Rumpelstiltskin was Phillip's guardian.*

CHAPTER 26

It took Phillip a month to recover fully. Lord Richtmann visited each day for the first two weeks. "Did you send a report to King Richard?" asked Ara as they watched the prince play quietly with his blocks.

"I did not. It would have taken weeks for the news to get to him. I only planned to let him know if...if the news necessitated his return." He faced his queen. "Fortunately, it did not. I see no reason to tell him now."

Minutes passed before Ara spoke. "Do you think Katerina acted alone? How would she have gotten the arsenic?"

"I am not sure," admitted the chancellor. "She came here from the service of Lord Alfred. It is possible he was behind the attempt. He is being watched carefully. A message about the nursemaid's suicide was sent to him, but nothing was mentioned about Phillip's poisoning. Your husband has had a good relation with his cousin, especially when Alfred's father was the regent when Richard was too young to rule. A king always has enemies. No one knows about the poisoning but the doctor and your family. It is best to keep it this way."

"I agree," said Ara, "but keep Alfred and Clotilde far away from Lundgrin."

CHAPTER 27

"Phillip! Phillip!" called Ara. "Wait up!"

The young prince reined his pony and waited for his mother to gallop up to him. He had promised to wait for her in the stables, but in his impishness, raced off towards the forest before she mounted her horse.

"That was very naughty," his mother chided when she caught up to him, trying to keep the amusement from her voice. They were at the edge of the deep woods. "Just because you are six years old, doesn't mean you can ride on without me."

The red-haired young boy laughed. "You are stuck riding sideways. I knew I could beat you to the trees." He was an easygoing boy who enjoyed a variety of physical activities. He and the servants' children regularly had running races and wrestled with each other besides using wooden swords on each other. His tutors informed Ara that he learned quickly, but was easily distracted. He wanted to use his body more than his brain.

"He is just a young boy," Ara defended. "You may have him for three hours a day, but then he must play with his toys and his mates. And he must have time to do one good deed every day." Good deeds were important to the queen. She knew her son would be a powerful king one day. She did not want him to forget he was a person just like all the others—just like she was—and he needed to be kind to all.

They rode into the shadows of the forest. The trees were leafing out, and the scent of new growth permeated the thick woods. "Stick to the paths," Ara cautioned. "There are brambles throughout, and I don't want you charging into them." She watched Phillip ride ahead, never going farther than her eyesight. He stopped and waited for her by her favorite tree and dismounted.

"Look," he said. "If I jump up, I can touch the leaves." He demonstrated for her.

"It will be no time before you are swinging from the branches." She examined the tree. "Maybe this year it will be old enough to grow acorns. Then it can feed other animals in the woods."

Steering the horses into the green meadows, they dismounted once again to see what creatures they could discover in the short, new grasses." They crouched about looking for bugs. Phillip was fascinated watching ants work together to carry a dead insect. Ara searched for spiders. She found a speckled cob weaving its web, and excitedly pointed out a daddy long legs to Phillip. "I'm not sure it's a true spider, because it only has one part to its body, not two like regular spiders." The bees were humming looking for early blooming flowers.

They were laying on their backs absorbing the sun's rays when Jana flew down to join them. "Can I hold him?" asked Phillip.

"Let's have you try. Sit on the ground."

As he sat cross-legged, Jana hopped into his lap, Phillip gently stroking his head. The raven quawed deep in his throat. "He likes me, Mama."

"Oh, Jana more than likes you. He watches over you to make sure you are safe. Maybe you are strong enough for him to sit on your shoulder. He's a big bird. Do you want to try?"

Phillip nodded. The young prince stood up while Jana climbed onto his shoulder. They were narrow, but Jana sat firmly in place, his head level with the prince's. "Phillip love," said the black bird. It was only the second time Jana said his name. Ara caught a sob in her throat thinking back to the first time.

"Yours is only the third name he has ever said."

Phillip furrowed his brow. "I know he says your name. What other name has he said?"

Ara rocked back and forth before answering. "He would say Amelie, my mother's name."

"He knew my grandmother?" His mouth dropped open, incredulous.

"He did. Tonight after you are tucked in bed, I will sit and tell you about him, but remember that Jana is our family's secret. Don't ever tell anyone about him. You would put him in danger."

Phillip looked at her solemnly with his blue and green eyes. "I will never tell anyone."

The next morning Frieda entered the apartment with her usual cheerful greeting. "Hello, love." She kissed Ara on each cheek. Ara caught the hollow look in her cousin's eyes. Frieda, who loved Phillip and her brother's daughters fiercely, was childless. Every month she hoped for a different outcome, but she was always disappointed. Now, after all these years, her dismay grew greater. Ara had no more encouraging words for her. "Please don't say anything," Frieda had begged holding up her hand. "I'm past hoping." No amount of prayers and countless candles lit in the church and the chapel changed the fact that Frieda remained barren.

Ara thought about the many times over the years she held Frieda in her arms while her cousin sobbed soundlessly. The only other person who knew her grief was Hans. It pained Ara to watch her dearest friend put forth a happy face while she grieved silently. Ara was determined to make Frieda's life as full and satisfying as possible. There was no one but Phillip she loved as dearly as her cousin.

The two of them continued to work in the flax fields with the peasants, and in the evenings, they spun and wove with the group of women who formed the guild many years ago. It was a simple life. The women laughed easily and told stories, some funny and others, including ghosts and murder, sent shivers sliding down their spines.

CHAPTER 28

Phillip turned eight when King Richard returned to Lundgrin Castle. Word had reached Ara that he would be returning within a week. Noblemen began arriving with their families and belongings, filling the castle once again. Servants were rehired and bustling about. Chambers, empty for years, were washed and dusted, and more food was prepared. Hunters, including Mannus, were sent out daily for fowl, boar, deer, conies and hares. The once quiet, serene life that Ara had become accustomed to was now interrupted by a whorl of people moving throughout the halls.

Pounding up the castle grounds on a magnificent steed, Richard made a show of his homecoming. Both the horse's mane and tail had been braided, and multicolored woolen blankets padded the polished saddle. The king wore an elaborate short purple silk tunic trimmed with a gold belt. Shiny spurs were on his high, leather boots. His long red hair had faded to the copper of autumn leaves. Behind him was a parade of twenty knights on horses as grand as his with their squires riding behind.

Ara and Phillip watched King Richard's arrival from a window several floors up. Phillip wanted to run to greet his father, but Chancellor Richtmann suggested that their reunion be private. They observed the king dismounting gingerly from his horse. He leaned on a squire and limped into the great hall as the courtiers who now occupied the castle greeted him with loud hales.

Richard kept court with his knights and noblemen. Sounds of raucous laughter and eating and drinking rang up to the higher floors, but not to the wing where Ara's apartment was. Music wafted through the castle for many evenings, but Richard did not come for Ara or his son. She kept to her rooms except to take early morning walks in the gardens rather than risk encountering him in the hallway. Phillip continued his lessons and played with his toys in his mother's chambers.

He was delighted when Marie brought her daughters to play with him, and Ara was happy for the company. Marie brought custard and gingerbread to the delight of the children. Ara and Frieda could not resist tasting the treats. The women sat and drew while Phillip patiently taught his cousins how to play chess. Growing bored, they tied up some of Ara's stockings into balls and took turns tossing them into a chalice. When his cousins left hours later, Phillip sat at his mother's feet. "Isn't father going to visit us?"

Ara was careful with her words. "Your father is a powerful man with many obligations. He must oversee the entire kingdom of Guendel which has expanded these last years. He has many men to meet with before he can come to see us. He has not forgotten you, and will be very surprised to see how you've grown." She tousled his hair. "He will think he is seeing a miniature of himself when at last the two of you meet. Be patient, my young son."

He crossed his arms in front of him and sighed. "I have been patient for many years, Mama."

It was a week before the king called for Ara and Phillip. They dressed carefully and waited to be summoned to his solar. Phillip sat with his hands beneath him, his legs swinging in the chair. Frieda answered a knock at the door, and the king's esquire entered. "King Richard will see you now," he announced stiffly.

Arising, mother and son followed him through passageways and up flights of stairs to Richard's apartment. The king was sitting facing the doorway when they entered. A broad smile filled his face when he saw his young son. "Phillip, you are the image of me when I was young," he declared. "Come closer. Let me look at you."

Phillip looked to his mother who indicated with a slight movement of her head to go to his father. He walked closer and bowed as he was taught. Richard clasped him by the shoulders and brought his son near to examine his face. "I have forgotten that you have my eyes, but in reverse. Your left eye is green and your right eye is blue." He laughed. "If a portrait were painted of you, that would be the only way people would know it was not I. Even your hair color is as red as mine was at your age. It should turn russet as you get to be a young man, just as mine has."

Deep furrowed lines were drawn down Richard's cheeks and across his forehead, his face red and dry. As the king sat his son on his lap, he winced in pain, and turned his attention to Ara. She had matured into a beautiful woman. She had been too angular and anxious when he last saw her, but now she appeared rounded and calm. It was too bad that he had already arranged to share his bed with one of the ladies for the evening. He would call for his queen another time. Perhaps he should be planning for another prince or a princess.

Richard had been away most of his son's life while conquering the lands to the northern seas and building a navy. He began marching his army to the west, but the kingdoms near the seas banded together, holding them at bay. His once small kingdom had grown, but at an enormous price. He lost many soldiers to death, injury, and desertion.

Some of the vanquished kingdoms were poorly tilled and had few valuable resources, making them easy enough to topple. The Knight Commander and regiments of soldiers were left behind to keep his new subjects from rebelling. The income from them was limited, but the cost to for their defense was large.

When the treasurer met with the king in his chambers, Richard was blunt. "I plan for another expedition to gain access to the western sea." He would need more knights and soldiers, war horses, archers, lances, catapults, and other war equipment.

The king had lost the little softness there was to him, and a cruel, hard crust had thickened on him causing the courtiers to become fearful of his outbursts. The treasurer wiped his brow. "Your Majesty, there are not enough coins and bullion to cover another undertaking."

"It cannot be so!" exploded Richard. "I had rooms full of gold bars and coins in my coffers, enough to last a lifetime. Take me to the treasury."

"I will take you, but the cost of the last expedition was enormous. You have been gone for nearly eight years. Just feeding a moving army is expensive, and then there are the costs of war horses, and equipment and the navy you are building."

They had reached the treasury, Richard limping along slowly. He examined the storage rooms. Two that had been filled with the melted strands from Ara's spinning were empty and the third was only half full. "Taxes, over time, will fill your coffers once again, if the money is spent sparingly, but it will take, perhaps, ten years. Another large expedition is not fathomable at this time."

Richard pondered the treasurer's statement. "I know a way," said the king.

CHAPTER 29

Ara longed for the Wednesday evenings in her chambers when her family would gather for meals and games. Frieda and Mannus made her laugh when they teased each other with quick-witted barbs. The children played quoits, or ran around in a game of tag or hide and seek. With the king and courtiers in the castle, she was forced to forgo this favorite family time.

"You look beautiful, but, come now, lift your shoulders. You are slumping forward," admonished Frieda. She had finished dressing Ara in a purple velvet gown that highlighted her blue eyes.

"Yes, I know, but these evening meals are noisy and boring. They would be more tolerable if Lord and Lady Belstrum were here. I hope he is well soon. His wife says he has an excess of black bile and bleeding him had not yet helped." Ara straightened her spine and forced a smile. "How is that?"

"I see a smile on your lips, but not in your eyes. That will do I suppose," replied Frieda, "but hurry. I do not want your husband to accuse me of making you late."

Ara walked down the dark hallways, the candles flickering on the walls, wishing she were in Belstrumburg spinning with her mother, her hand dipping into the cup of water to keep the flax from sticking to her fingers. As she turned corners and walked down staircases, the sounds of voices became louder until they reached a crescendo. She entered the great hall.

The next day Phillip rushed into Ara's chambers with Jana cradled in his arms. "Mama, quick, come here," he called. Ara hurried from her bedchamber to the anteroom. "Jana's been injured."

Tenderly Ara took the bird's limp body into her arms. "His wing is broken and he's bleeding." She brought him to a table. Jana croaked loudly when she touched his belly. "What happened?"

"My friends and I were using pine cones as targets for our slingshots. Lord Dussel's son saw Jana overhead and shot him. I didn't even know it happened until Jana fell from the sky." He began crying big heaving sobs. "Is he going to die?"

"I don't know," she worried. "Let's hope not. Get me a cloth from the privy chamber. I have some wine. I will clean his wound." Together they tended to the raven. "We should move him to the wardrobe room to keep him away from prying eyes. I do not want any of the ladies who visit me or your father to know he is here." Phillip made him a nest from a smock and gently rested him in it. "His leg looks broken. We'll fashion him a splint." Phillip went to the garden and retrieved a small twig that he whittled down, and Ara tied it to Jana's leg with thread. "We have done all we can. Now we shall see what time will do for Jana."

When Jana fell asleep, Ara encouraged Phillip to go out to play. She sat alone in the room with Jana, tears spilling from her eyes. *Do not die, my sweet friend,* she pleaded silently. *Do not die.*

Frieda brought him fish and and nuts from the kitchen each day. "He's getting stronger. Do you think he will be able to fly again?"

"I do not know. His appetite is returning, but he cannot walk. He hasn't even tried to move his wing. We can hope."

CHAPTER 30

"Mama says you are a powerful king and that is why you had to be away for many years." Phillip was sitting on his father's lap in Richard's solar while Ara sat close by.

The king's voice was deep and booming. "When I inherited the throne," he exaggerated to his son, "Guendel was but a small, poor kingdom. We had sheep and a few crops in the fields, rivers but no outlet to the sea. This castle and its surroundings were its only great measure of the land. Over these last fifteen years, I have conquered many kingdoms making my way to the northern sea. I am determined to make my way to the western sea and have the greatest navy in the world."

"You will make the kingdom even larger?" asked Phillip.

"One day I will leave you an empire that spans from here to the sea in the north and the lands that form its western shores. I expect you to grow it to the mountains to the east and down to the southern coast. History will remember me as a powerful leader, but you will be even greater."

Phillip jumped from his father's lap and pushed out his chest. "I will be a great king!" he shouted.

"Not king. Emperor!" roared Richard, laughing. Ara frowned. She did not like the influence the king had on her son.

Ara asked to meet privately with Lord Richtmann. "Did you ever tell Richard about Phillip's poisoning?" she questioned.

They were in his chamber in another wing of the castle. The heavy drapes covering the windows were open and the shutters had been pushed against the recess of the wall allowing the morning sunlight to stream in. The chancellor sat behind a large mahogany desk. Ara perched lightly in front of it, her hands folded in her lap. "Since it appeared to be caused by a deranged woman acting alone, I saw no reason to remark upon it. I still have Alfred and Clotilde being watched, but there have never been signs of their involvement. It is interesting that they have not come to Lundgrin to see Richard now that he has returned. They are clever, though, so I do not trust them thoroughly. It will only raise the king's ire and cause him distress if you tell him about it now. I would advise against it."

"I agree with your sentiments, Chancellor. The king seems rather..." Ara searched for a word, "high strung right now. I am concerned that it is because he has been injured, although he does not speak of it."

"Three years ago, the steed he was riding in combat was mortally wounded. As it fell, Richard landed under it. His left hip and knee received much damage. He needed to be carried from the field. He is much improved, but I do not think they can be corrected further. No one mentions his injury. He is sensitive about his impairment."

"I shall not reference it, and I have instructed Phillip to do likewise. Thank you for the information." The chancellor bowed as Ara left. She walked back to her chambers feeling unsettled. Richard had only returned to Lundgrin Castle twice in eight years, and both times he had been injured in war. Why did he need to keep expanding the kingdom? Why was he not satisfied with the riches that he has?

Ara saw little of Richard during the day, but he came to her chambers late each evening. "We should expand our family to ensure my dynasty endures." She was relieved that he never spent the night, but stayed only as long as necessary. Her husband was not much more than a stranger to her, and though she did not like having him in her bed, she liked the thought of having another child.

Richard was getting dressed after leaving Ara's bed. "I am going off to visit all of Guendel. It is time that I see how the kingdom is fairing, and the citizens should be reminded of their king."

He had been back at Lundgrin for more than a month and was growing restless.

"How long will you be away?"

"A month or two. In the meantime, I have left orders for Phillip to begin lessons in swordsmanship."

"He is young for that, is he not?"

"No, he is not!" Richard's voice rose in irritation. "I began lessons when I was younger than he is now. You are coddling him. He will be king one day. I will take him with me when I go on my next conquest."

Ara had been laying back on her pillow, but now she bolted upright. "You are going to take Phillip off to war?"

"Yes, he can serve as my page and later my squire. By the time I return from touring Guendel, he will have learned the basics of swordsmanship, and my knights can teach him finer details while he is with me on my expedition west."

"He has lessons here. He is being tutored in history, geography, and philosophy." Ara was trying to keep a rising panic from her voice.

"If he is to be a conqueror, he needs to know how to fight. I will show him how a great king leads. That is more important than the lessons being taught here."

"Fighting is dangerous. You have been injured fighting in your wars. He is too young for an expedition of this sort." Her voice was getting higher.

Richard leaned close to her face. "Life itself is dangerous," he sneered. "Woman, you do not tell me what is best for my son. I say he is going off with me, and that is final."

Ara swallowed a sob. She knew it meant she would not see her son for years. He might return injured, or he might not return at all. Her face grew hot as anger and helplessness filled her.

He had finished dressing and pulled keys from the pouch on his belt. "I need you to spin gold for me again. I have had the rooms where you spun before filled with straw. Do not go in during the daytime when others may see you."

Ara jumped from the bed, standing with her arms open at her sides, palms forward. She began shaking, her legs weakening. "I cannot. It is a skill I have long forgotten."

Richard limped back to her, his eyes as cold as steel. Grabbing her by the back of her head, his fingers entwined in her hair, he spit out his words. "You have lived in this castle for fifteen years, being bowed to, wearing clothes of silk and velvet, and having your food served on silver plates. I did not make you queen for you to tell me you can no longer spin gold. You will spin every day that I am gone." He threw the keys on the bed. "These will open the rooms. If they are not filled with gold when I return, I will cut you to pieces slowly, one finger at a time, one leg at a time, until there is nothing left of you but the blue of your eyes."

Moving his hand to her face, he pushed her to the floor, and hobbled from the apartment. Ara lay there trembling, her heartbeats pounding and irregular. This was the man she had been forced to marry, the one she knew would have killed her if she refused all those years ago. She needed to get away from him, but what escape was there? She could never leave Phillip. She lay there for hours, too frightened to move, arising only as the sky began to lighten. She could not let her cousin see her like this.

Sounds of horses, voices, and furniture being loaded into carriages filled the morning and afternoon. Men were giving orders and women were gathering their children, saying goodbyes to each other. Richard had left with his entourage in the early hours of the morning to inspect the kingdom. He would stay with Alfred and then at the manors of his lords and a few of his lesser castles while he was gone. With the king away, the courtiers had no reason to remain.

Ara did not leave her bedchamber for most of the day, feigning illness. She carried Jana from the wardrobe and kept him near her side. In the late afternoon she went into the antechamber. "Frieda, I am going out alone to my father's grave, and on for a walk," she said somberly. "Stay here if you would like, or go to visit Marie. Fresh air may do me some good."

She slipped on her cloak and treaded dejectedly down the stairs to the outside. She stood wordlessly in front of Peter's cross. *I am lost,* she thought. *I became trapped fifteen years ago, but the snare did not bite hard until now. I will be with you and Mama soon, but I cannot bear to leave Phillip to a dangerous fate.*

Dreading the thought of walking back into the castle, the edifice that had been like a prison to her, she ambled into the woods, letting her hands trail through the branches of the bushes along the path. When she reached her tree, she slid to the forest floor, her back against the trunk. She wrapped her arms around her legs, and let her head rest against her knees. Her sobs racked her body until she was spent. Slowly, she rose from the ground, wiping her eyes with her hands. As she turned to leave, a small cold object brushed against her forehead. She looked up, and hanging from a low branch was her mother's necklace, the letter A catching the little light left of the day. She pulled it from the branch and placed it around her neck and under her smock.

Rumpelstiltskin is nearby, she thought. *Surely, this is a message. Perhaps he will spin straw into gold for me again.* She unclasped the brooch that kept a lock of Phillip's hair, the one Richard had given her when she gave birth to the prince. She removed it from the placket of her gown, placed it in the crotch of the tree, and hurried back to the her apartment.

"The sun sets early these days," she remarked to Frieda upon her return. "I have yet to get used to the temperature dropping so rapidly when the sun goes down." Her face was flushed with hope.

"You seem to be feeling better. Your walk outside seems to have done you some good," commented Frieda.

"More than you know."

CHAPTER 31

Nearing midnight, Ara's room was cold and dim, only two candles lighting the chamber. The flickering lights cast shadows across the walls and on the ceiling. She had been sitting, fully dressed, for hours, Only the wringing of her hands in her lap betrayed her nervousness. A movement caught her eye by the fireplace, first a small light and then, fully fleshed, stood Rumpelstiltskin.

"You have come, good man," she whispered. "I knew you would."

Rumpelstiltskin bowed. "Once again you are in danger, Miss Miller."

Her lips twitched at the mention of her name. "You have been watching me."

"I have watched out for you all these years," acknowledged the small man, "trying to keep you from danger."

"You saved Phillip by speaking to the doctor."

"I almost failed. By the time I reached him, he had already ingested some poison. The only way to stop his nursemaid from feeding him more was to throw her from the balcony."

"She did not jump?"

"No."

Ara was silent for a moment. "The king demands that I spin straw into gold. Can you do it once again for me?"

"I cannot. The skill is not within me any longer."

Ara got down on her knees. "Then, sir, I am dead, and the king will take Phillip into battle poorly armed. My son will be killed." She held Rumpelstiltskin's eyes steady. "Take us with you, Phillip and me. You wanted a child. Better that you have him than let him die in battle. I will serve you. I will cook and clean and farm for you, whatever you need."

Rumpelstiltskin did not speak at once. "I cannot take you. You are fully grown and too large to vanish with me. I can only take Phillip."

Ara's shoulders sagged and she rested her head on the seat of her chair. "I see. That is my fate." She raised her head. "Very well. I will give you Phillip tomorrow. If you take him now, innocent servants will be arrested when it is discovered that he is missing. I will bring him to the tree where you found my brooch before daylight falls."

Rumpelstiltskin assented. "It is agreed."

"One more thing." Ara rose and walked swiftly from the room. She returned carrying Jana. "Take him with you. This raven will be a comfort to Phillip in his new home. He is injured and cannot fly." She kissed her old friend and told him to watch over her son, and then placed him gently in Rumpelstiltskin's arms.

"I will care for him as if he were my own." With a nod, he faded away into the air.

CHAPTER 32

"It is brisk outside this morning," Frieda said as she entered the antechamber. "Autumn is fickle, warm one day and cold the next." She put down the cider she was carrying and unbuttoned her mantle, removing it in one sweeping motion. "Here, sit with me," she said handing Ara a cup. "It's warm and will take the chill out of you."

Ara sat down next to her cousin. There was an aura of calm around her. Her fate had been set; she would face it stoically. Frieda chatted on. "Only two noble families remain in the castle, and they will be gone before the afternoon. I saw the carriages out in the courtyard as I arrived."

"It will be peaceful once again around here," lied Ara, knowing the chaos that would be created once Phillip was gone. She looked at Frieda. She was a little fuller in the middle, but otherwise she had changed little since she arrived to serve Ara those many years ago. There were lines around her eyes, but they were from crinkling with merriment. She laughed easily, showing her dimples.

"None of the temporary kitchen helpers or servants remain. The castle steward swiftly eliminated them from the staff." Frieda kept her hands around the cup, warming them. "We should start up our spinning group again. The women have asked about it, and I told them that once Lundgrin was absent of guests, the queen will want to begin again."

"You know me well," Ara put down her cider. "Help me get dressed. I want to look especially nice for Phillip today."

They went into the wardrobe together. Frieda looked around. "Where is Jana?"

"I should have started the morning telling you the good news. Jana flew off. He will be back tomorrow. He always is here at daybreak." Lies were building upon lies.

"Good morning, Phillip," Ara greeted her son. She was sitting lightly on his bed watching him as he became fully awake.

"Good morning, Mama." Phillip smiled and stretched. "You are a good surprise."

"Today is a day of surprises." Ara's voice caught in her throat. *No, no more tears. The decision has been made.* "It is a day of freedom for us. Let us think of all the fun things we want to do, just the two of us, and we will see how many we can make happen." She smiled and stroked his face. "Up with you. I have your favorite breakfast waiting."

Phillip could not believe his good luck. His mother said no to nothing. They went to the stable for their horses, and rode through the meadows and even down near the fields, waving to the peasants who returned the wave. He took her to the butts where he made his mother try archery. He laughed with glee at her ineptitude. "You should have made Mannus teach you," he howled. Next he got out stilts and and showed off his skill at walking with them. He insisted that she try, but she could not even stand up on them.

They had a picnic in the tall grass. Ara showed him how to trample down the thin stalks to make a place for them to sit. She told him stories of her home in Belstrumburg and how her father once convinced her that she had seen a whale. "He was such a good storyteller," she recalled, shaking her head.

Phillip was good in quoits, tossing more rings on the stake than his mother, but she bested him in queek. "Let's play Blind Man's Bluff," she suggested. They tramped forward to the edge of the forest. Not many of the leaves had dropped, and there was still green showing through the yellow and red and orange splatters hanging on the trees. Ara let her eyes absorb all the colors. She wanted her last memory of her son to be filled with beauty.

"Actually, I have a surprise for you in the woods. There is a man, a good man, I want you to meet."

"Where is he?"

"Be patient. You will see him soon enough." They entered the woods and walked along the familiar path.

"There he is!" shouted Phillip. "He is standing right next to our tree." He turned to Ara. "He is little."

"Yes, he is a small man, but do not judge him by his size."
They walked up to meet him. "Phillip, I would like you to
meet Rumpelstiltskin."

"Good day to you, sir." Phillip held out his hand.

Rumpelstiltskin looked much as before, but had traded his
short mantle for a long cloak. "I am pleased to meet you." He
took the prince's hand and shook it. "What a fine boy you are."

Ara knelt by Phillip. "Rumpelstiltskin will take you on a
wonderful adventure."

His eyes widened. "Where will we go?"

"I will show you in just a moment," replied the small man.
"First, a word with your mother." He took Ara aside. "I will
not abandon you. Tonight the moon will be full. Escape to the
woods. I cannot help you with that, but once you have broken
free, I will lead you to me. I move from place to place, but I will
remain where I am until you find me. Head north, traveling
only at night. I am a two days' journey away, but well hidden.
Once you find me, we will be safe to travel on together."

"How will you lead me? asked Ara. "Will you come
for me?"

"I cannot, but you will have help from our fellow spinners
and weavers. The spiders of the forest will guide you. Look up
to find your way." He lifted her hand and rubbed her wheat
ring, spinning it around on her finger. "This ring will pinch
your finger if there is peril. Heed its warning."

Ara nodded.

222

"I have a gift for you." He handed her a finely woven black shawl. "This is made of spider webbing. Strand for strand it is stronger than steel, but is as light as air. You will find it useful."

"Thank you, my friend." She walked back to her son. "You are safe with Rumpelstiltskin. He has many treats planned, and one final surprise is that Jana will be waiting for you when you get to where you're going. I will join you in two days."

Phillip hugged his mother. "Thank you for this day. It has been the best one yet. I will see you soon." He stood next to Rumpelstiltskin coming past his shoulders.

"Say hello to Jana for me. I will see you in two days."

Rumpelstiltskin wrapped his cloak around Phillip, and then pulling his hood over his head, they disappeared.

CHAPTER 33

In a blink, they disappeared. Not a fading or a shiver or a wavering in the air, but a vanishing. A shudder of fear snaked down her spine. She had taken a chance with her son's life and could only hope she was right.

Ara unlaced her gown, threw it to the ground and stomped on it. She loosened the laces on her kirtle and slipped the shawl into its side to hide it. She rubbed dirt onto the kirtle, smock, and her face. Looking around, she found a hand-sized rock and hit herself about her eyes and cheeks with it until she drew blood. *There,* she thought. *I will look properly bruised.*

Next Ara donned and laced her gown. She scratched her arms and face, and, finally, she took off her coif and pulled strands from her plaits. Taking two deep breaths to steady herself, she began her run from the forest. As she emerged from its fringe, she began shouting and flailing her arms.

"My son! My son! Help me! He has been taken!" she shouted. She knew her voice wouldn't carry to the castle yet, but she wanted it hoarse and cracking by the time she reached the guards. They saw Ara before they heard her and ran out to meet her. By the time they reached her, she was breathless and near to collapse from the run. It was easy to show distress because she had just taken the biggest chance of her life, of Phillip's life.

"Your Majesty," spoke the senior of the three, "speak calmly and tell us what has happened."

Taking gulping breaths, Ara spoke. "Two men on horseback accosted us in the woods. They grabbed Phillip and pushed me down. I tried grabbing him, but they knocked me about the face and threw me back. I fell again. Phillip began screaming in terror, and one of them hit him until he fell silent." She began sobbing, her hands covering her face. "They were too strong and fast for me. Go after them! Get Phillip back!"

"You must settle yourself if we are to help you," the head guard admonished. "Did you recognize them?"

"No." She began to quiet down, "they spoke in a strange language. Their clothing was unfamiliar, too. I have never seen these men before."

"Were they peasants or soldiers?"

"Perhaps soldiers from a different kingdom, definitely not common men."

"Which way did they go?"

"They were heading west, towards the sun." Ara began moaning. "Hurry," she implored them. "Gather your men and go after them. You must get Phillip back."

"Escort her back to the castle, and meet us at the stables," instructed the leader. He turned to the other. "Get three men and tell them to prepare for a search. I will let the chancellor know."

Ara allowed the guard to escort her to her apartment, but insisted he leave her at the door. Frieda rushed to her when she saw her cousin's state. "What happened? Did you fall?" She drew Ara to a chair. "Let me clean you up." She rose to get cloths, but Ara restrained her, holding her arm.

She searched Frieda's face. "Listen carefully to me. Phillip has been taken by strange men."

Frieda gasped and jumped up, knocking over the chair. "Not our Phillip. It cannot be! Who took him?"

"Two men on horses. They grabbed him and knocked me down." Ara lied easily knowing Frieda's life depended on it as well as her own. "The guards are readying a search. I need your help. Go to the kitchen and bring me dried foods, figs, apples, meats, whatever you can find."

"Are you going in search of Phillip? The guards will not allow it."

Ara grasped her into an embrace. "Do not ask me any questions, Frieda. It is dangerous to ask questions. You do not want to know the answers."

When her cousin hurried from the room, Ara changed into her peasant clothes, stuffing the shawl under her kirtle. She strode into her bedchamber and, using her teeth, she began ripping the top bedsheet into strips. When Frieda returned, she stared at the torn sheet, dropping the dried foods on a table. "What are you doing?"

"Sit down with me." Ara pulled two chairs so they sat facing each other. "Before he left, Richard threatened to kill me when he returns." Frieda began to speak, but Ara put up her hand to stop her. "He will do it. I must leave now. You are in danger because no one is closer to me than you. If I do not make my leaving look like a kidnapping, Richard will surely take your head off."

"Are you meeting up with Phillip? Where will you go?"

Ara shook her head. "Ask me nothing, my darling cousin." She hesitated before she spoke again. "I will have to tie you up to ensure you look like you had no part in my disappearance."

Frieda took Ara's hands and they leaned towards each other touching foreheads, wordless. Frieda lifted her head. "You must give me half an hour," she said, and ran out the door.

Ara tied pouches with the dried food and skins of wine around her waist and was knocking over furniture when Frieda reentered the apartment. "Here is some rope," she said, taking a long length from a sack she carried. "Tie me with this instead. Kidnappers would have come prepared and would not have taken time to rip sheets. We must remake the bed," she ordered, taking a fresh sheet from the sack. They finished the task quickly. Next she pulled out servant attire. "A peasant would not be in the castle in the evening. Put this on over your clothing." She helped Ara dress. "Here are two more items. "This jar contains pig's blood. I stole it from the kitchen. Pour it over my head so I will look badly injured. And here." She handed Ara a cudgel. "Drop it next to me when you leave."

Ara drew back. "I cannot hurt you."

"If you do not hurt me, the king will. You must, Ara. It is a proper weapon. I will look like a victim, not an accomplice."

"We must hurry. I must be gone by dark and I have heard the nightjar calling."

"You mean the goatsucker." The two women looked at each other and smiled. "I love you, Ara Miller."

"I love you, Frieda Cooper." She began to tie her up, first her hands behind her back, and then her feet. When Frieda lay down on the floor, she tied her feet to her hands, and grabbed the cudgel.

"Do it quickly."

Ara looked up and closed her eyes. Raising the weapon, she brought it down on her cousin's head. Frieda grunted and her head fell forward, her body motionless. A small stream of blood began to trickle from her wound. Quickly, she dropped the cudgel and poured the pig's blood on Frieda's hair. She put her hand to Frieda's chest and felt the strong, rhythmic beating of her heart. She gathered up the torn sheet and the jar, and stuffed them into the sack. Then she adjusted the coif low over her forehead and hurried out the door.

With the courtiers and the king gone from the castle, there were few people about. It was easy to scurry down the hallways and stairs. Ara looked like every other female servant, and the guards were not concerned with them. She was able to slip out the gate easily. She forced herself to walk at a normal pace down the path she had walked hundreds of times over the years and headed toward the fields. When she got to the high grasses, she crept in among them and discarded the servant uniform and the sack.

Ara was fearful that her solitary figure could be seen from the castle battlements, so she slunk slowly through the gorse and high grasses towards the northern edge of the forest. The breeze waving the stalks helped hide her movements. High, thin clouds streaked across the full moon in an otherwise clear sky. It was only when she stepped into the trees did she realize she had been taking shallow breaths. She inhaled deeply as she felt a measure of safety among the cover of the trees.

Rumpelstiltskin had promised a path, but there were no markings on the ground. A shiver of fear that he had cruelly tricked her began to snake down her spine. *No,* she thought shaking the idea from her mind, *he said to look up.* She tilted her head back, and there she caught a glinting in the trees. Glistening spider webs were strung throughout the treetops showing her the trail.

Relief rushed through her and, focusing on the path above, she hastened at a hare's pace over the moss and detritus that covered the forest floor. It wasn't long before her foot snagged a tree root and she stumbled hard to the ground. She let out a low moan and rose slowly rubbing her knee and blotting the blood from the scrapes on her elbows. *Keep careful and steady,* she thought as she began anew, at a slower speed, limping her way and attending more to the ground.

The moon moved halfway across the sky before Ara stopped to rest, crouching against an old sycamore. The air had cooled and the crickets had stopped chirruping. The forest was silent except for the occasional hooting of a distant owl. She swallowed some wine, and stood, shivering. Taking the spider-woven shawl from beneath her bodice, she wrapped it around her shoulders, letting it trail around the skirt of her kirtle. It was lightweight but warming. She gave a silent thanks to Rumpelstiltskin and moved on.

As a cacophony of wakening birds began rising through the forest, Ara's steps began to falter. Searching around for a hiding place, she spied a large, deep crevice a foot off the ground in a rotting beech. She wedged her tired body inside, inhaling the moist aroma of decaying wood. Removing her pouch of food from her belt, she nibbled on jerky and dried apples, and took a long pull of wine. Settling in, she draped the black shawl completely over her, and cocooned inside, she fell into an exhausted sleep.

The sun was casting slanting shadows by the time the chittering sounds of the woodland aroused Ara from sleep. Slowly she unfolded herself from her hiding place and stretched. Her body ached from her awkward sleeping position and last night's long journey. Her throbbing knee was hot to the touch. There were still a few hours of daylight remaining before it was safe enough to travel. Looking around, she found some blackberries dried on their branches to add to her evening meal. She rested against the sheltering beech as she chewed her food looking out at her surroundings.

The mixed forest looked different from the one close to the castle. Here were more beeches, tall and thick with long crooked roots covered with low plants. Their dark green oval leaves had turned shades of yellow, orange and a coppery brown. Large rocks lay scattered among the trees and bushes, and the ground undulated like the waves in the river by the mill. Stately pines and spruce dominated the woods, carpeting the floor with old needles and cones. The heavy scent of pine hung in the air.

A fallow deer walked into view, its antlers nodding as it grazed peacefully. When a sudden screech of a jay startled it, the white spots on its back rippled as it flexed its hind quarters and bounded off.

As the sky darkened, Ara kept her gaze at the forest canopy waiting for the spider webs to shimmer. Her ears were perked for the sounds of horse hooves or the snapping of branches, but all she heard were the goo goo cry of a dove and the din of frogs calling out. Finally, the glimmering of webs appeared. "Thank you, Rumpelstiltskin," she whispered. Retying her provisions onto her belt, she set off once more.

Her knee ached as she walked throughout the evening. Her webbed shawl loosely wrapped around her shoulders and her steady speed kept her warm despite the steady drop in temperature. The shimmering cobwebs above her were a reassuring comfort.

The moon traveled east across the sky. As she ventured deeper into the woods, she reached a section filled with oaks; the underbrush was thick and her travel slowed. A sharp pinch of her ring brought her to a stop. Danger! Quickly she scanned around for safety, and spying low branches on a nearby tree, she threw an end of her shawl around a limb and pulled herself up before climbing to a higher limb.

Three silver gray wolves trotted into view, then slowed and put their long snouts to the ground. Their neck hair and hackles rose as they sniffed around the tree, her scent detected. She sat on the branch, still as a stone. Finding nothing, they sauntered off, but the ring continued to pinch. It wasn't long before the wolves circled back, nosed about, and, finally, loped away. When Ara's finger stopped throbbing, she cautiously climbed down. Spying the spiders' trail, she resumed her trek.

When the glow of the sun erased the moon, Ara searched around for a place to rest. Fearful of another wolf encounter, she decided her safest place was off the ground. She climbed as high as she dared in a tree and tied the ends of the shawl to sturdy branches to form a hammock. She nestled in, and finding it surprisingly comfortable, she fell asleep.

CHAPTER 34

Ara awoke with a start. Her ring was pinching her finger hard. Soon she heard the sounds of horses and men in the distance. She turned her body in the direction of the voices, staring at leaves inches from her face. She held her breath as they passed beneath her. Two horses plodded along as the soldiers astride them scanned the forest. She tried to determine the direction they were traveling, but she could not see the sun. She could only hope it was not north.

At last the ring eased and Ara descended from the tree, snagging her kirtle in the twigs. A sharp pain jolted her when she touched the ground. She lifted her skirt and gasped. Her injured knee was twice the size of the other. She hobbled about until she found a broken branch to use as a walking stick. The moon had risen and was sharing the sky with the sun. In an hour, the sun would be vanquished and the lunar orb would be the master of the heavens.

I could have met up with Rumpelstiltskin and Phillip by now, if I had not injured my knee, she thought. She prayed she would reach them tonight. Her damaged leg would only allow her to limp at a slow, shuffling pace. Ara looked at the webbed trail, shambled forward, rested, and moved along again. Hours passed. Despite the cool night, she was sweating from her efforts. She came across a stream and splashed her face and rested. Then she moved on.

The trees thinned out and the glistening webs trailed to the ground. Ara had reached a long, wide meadow. She could see that the twinkling along the grasses disappeared to blackness ahead. *What can this mean?* She doddered forward as quickly as she dared. The meadow was soggy and water seeped through her shoes. As she came closer to the inky emptiness, she heard fast running water. She could make out a gorge roughly twenty cubits wide and the webs glimmering on the other side. When she reached its edge, she could see a river rushing below. She needed to cross the chasm but, looking left and right, she could see no place to cross.

She felt despair rising within her, but she tamped it down. There had to be a way over. Rumpelstiltskin had led her with the spider webs, and he had given her ring the power to warn of danger. The answer had to be in the shawl. It had served no special purpose so far. She removed it from her shoulders and set it on the ground to examine it. It must hold some power to help her now.

As the sky lightened, Ara saw movement at the bottom of the grasses. She lowered her face and saw thousands of spiders of all different colors and sizes crawling towards her. Some, as large as her palm, and others, like specks of dust, climbed over and around her, halting when they came to the shawl. In unison, they began dragging it to the verge of the gorge. After they fastened it to an outcropping of rocks, they spun out long strings of silk that reached the other side. After securing those strands, they pulled at the shawl, stretching it until it reached the opposite rim. The shawl's tight weave had lengthened to form a bridge.

Fear was consuming her, but the shiny webs on the other side lured her forward. She was close to Phillip now. It was impossible for her to walk across with her injured knee. Making a sign of the cross, she lowered herself on all fours, and began pulling herself forward .

The sun was glowing above the horizon and she was not yet across. The soldiers emerged from the forest and watched from afar. "Is that a person or an animal crossing a bridge?" one asked. They spurred their horses across the meadow. Ara heard rather than saw the horses galloping closer. Wincing with pain, she hurried across the last cubit of the bridge. Wheeling around, she saw it disintegrate into millions of strands that floated to the waters below. Quickly she flattened herself against the ground, concealing herself in the tall grass.

The soldiers dismounted when they reached the gorge. They could see the rushing water below, but there was no sign of a bridge. "Did we imagine something walking across this divide?"

"I thought I saw it emerge on the other side and disappear."

The first soldier shook his head. "It is impossible. There are no makings of a bridge here at all. It must have been a sorceress bewitching our minds. Let us keep on the edge of the forest until we find a path east and look there. We will meet up with the others and continue searching with them." They mounted their horses, and giving the gorge a final look, turned and trotted off towards the forest.

It took Ara an hour before she dared to move. When she tried to stand, she muffled a scream. Her knee would not hold her. Crossing the bridge on all fours had damaged it even further. She crumpled to the ground and writhed in pain. She would wait for nightfall before setting out again. Curling herself up into a ball and covering her eyes with her coif, she slept fitfully.

Nighttime had long fallen before Ara tried to stand, but failed. She tore strips off the bottom of her smock and wrapping her knees and hands to pad them, she began dragging and crawling forward trying not to touch her injured knee to the ground, while keeping her eyes on the winking spider webs. When she reached the edge of the woods, she searched until she found another branch that would be sturdy enough to serve as a walking stick. She rose up and managed to trudge forward by holding it with two hands.

She hobbled on until the smell of venison drifted past her nose. Frightened, she froze, but her ring remained still. Cautiously, she continued forward, the aroma of food getting stronger. Finally, she entered a clearing where two figures stood by a fire, one of them slowly stirring a pot hanging above it.

Phillip turned. "Mama," he cried, "you are here!" and ran to her. She grabbed him with one arm, but began teetering to one side. He caught her and he and Rumpelstiltskin lifted her to the fire.

They sat her down carefully, letting her one leg stretch out. Ara held her son, stroking his hair and murmuring his name.

"I knew you would be here tonight," said Rumpelstiltskin as he scooped some stew into a bowl. "Eat," he urged. When she refused to let her son out of her arms, he fed her each spoonful.

Later he helped Ara to a cabin tucked into a thicket. She sunk into a bed in a tiny nook off to one side. There she slept a full night and day.

When she awoke, she found Phillip by her side. Both smiled at one another. "Welcome back, Mama." She squeezed his hand.

Jana flew to her, his wings folding smoothly at his sides. She nuzzled him. "You are better, my friend."

Rumpelstiltskin entered the cabin. "Good to see you awake."

Ara's smile faded. "Frieda."

"She is safe and well. No one suspects her. She is resting at home with her husband. Now, let us get some food into you."

CHAPTER 35

Ara, Phillip, and Rumpelstiltskin lived quietly in the cabin for months. As her knee slowly mended, she began working alongside them scavenging for nuts and fruits and trapping animals. In the evening she and Rumpelstiltskin took turns spinning and weaving while Phillip read or strummed a lute.

Jana no longer flew away each night, instead spending all his time with the three of them. They happily fed him as he took turns sitting next to each of them in the evenings. During the day he flew into the trees nearby or traveled on one of their shoulders.

One evening as they sat around the outside fire, Phillip pointed to his mother's hand. "What is the design on your ring?"

Ara removed it and handed it to her son. "This gold ring is in the shape of wheat. My father gave it to my mother. He must have worked long and hard to have earned the money for it. "

He examined it closely. "It's delicate and finely made," he said handing it back to her.

She unclasped the necklace and handed it to him. "He gave her this necklace, too. It has her initial on it, A for Amelie, but she gave it to me the year I turned twelve. Now it is an A for Ara."

Phillip rubbed the pendant disc with his finger feeling its smoothness before turning it over. "It is beautiful as well, but there is a small flaw in the back."

Ara took it and brought the necklace up to her eyes. "I never noticed this tiny groove before. It has always sat facing forward on my neck. Perhaps it was somehow damaged on my journey to you."

"No," spoke Rumpelstiltskin as he took the necklace from Ara's hands. He plucked a thorn from a nearby bush. Placing its point into the groove, the pendant sprung open, revealing a second disc behind the first. He handed the necklace back to Ara.

She studied the second disc and looked up at Rumpelstiltskin. "It has an R on it."

"I made her the necklace and the ring."

Ara sprung up, her hand to her mouth. "You knew my mother? How can that be?"

"I knew her since she was a child. We were inseparable. We found an injured bird..."

"You were the friend that helped her nurse Jana back to health?" She paced around, unbelieving.

Rumpelstiltskin nodded. "Sit, Ara, and I will tell you the story of your mother and me."